Z

Treasure

Other Penny Spring and Sir Toby Glendower Mysteries

MARGOT ARNOLD

Zadok's Treasure

A Penny Spring and Sir Toby Glendower Mystery

Foul Play Press

The Countryman Press
Woodstock, Vermont

This edition is published in 1989 by Foul Play Press, an imprint
of The Countryman Press, Inc., Woodstock, Vermont 05091.

ISBN 0-88150-133-6

Printed in the United States of America

TO MARGARET AND JOHN COOPER,
GOOD FRIENDS AND GENTLE PEOPLE

WHO'S WHO

GLENDOWER, TOBIAS MERLIN, archaeologist, F.B.A., F.S.A., K.B.E.; b. Swansea, Wales, Dec. 27, 1926; s. Thomas Owen and Myfanwy (Williams) G.; ed. Winchester Coll.; Magdalen Coll., Oxford, B.A., M.A., Ph.D.; fellow Magdalen Coll., 1949-; prof. Near Eastern and European Prehistoric Archaeology Oxford U., 1964-; created Knight, 1977. Participated in more than 30 major archaeological expeditions. Author publications, including: What Not to Do in Archaeology, 1960; What to Do in Archaeology, 1970; also numerous excavation and field reports. Clubs: Old Wykehamists, Athenaeum, Wine-tasters, University.

SPRING, PENELOPE ATHENE, anthropologist; b. Cambridge, Mass., May 16, 1928; d. Marcus and Muriel (Snow) Thayer; B.A., M.A., Radcliffe Coll.; Ph.D., Columbia U.; m. Arthur Upton Spring, June 24, 1953 (dec.); 1 son, Alexander Marcus. Lectr. anthropology Oxford U., 1958-68; Mathieson Reader in anthropology Oxford U., 1969-; fellow St. Anne's Coll., Oxford, 1969-. Field work in the Marquesas, East and South Africa, Uzbekistan, India, and among the Pueblo, Apache, Crow and Fox Indians. Author: Sex in the South Pacific, 1957; The Position of Women in Pastoral Societies, 1962; And Must They Die? — A Study of the American Indian, 1965; Caste and Change, 1968; Moslem Women, 1970; Crafts and Culture, 1972; The American Indian in the Twentieth Century, 1974; Hunter vs. Farmer, 1976.

CHAPTER 1

"Bill has disappeared. I just know something has happened—he never would have gone off like that. You *must* help me find him." The pale spring light, filtering in through the small jungle of green plants sitting on the sill of the large office window, cast a greenish glow over the pallid features of the woman who spoke, giving her the appearance of a messenger from some eerie, lightless world.

Sir Tobias Glendower, barricaded behind his large desk with its toppling masses of papers, archaeological journals and a general mishmash of antiquities, looked with marked distaste at his unwelcome visitor, seated in the chair on the other side of the desk. Everything about her was so pale; her ash-blonde hair and white eyelashes fringing the light gray eyes, the blanched-looking skin, the pale pink thin-lipped mouth that now drooped disconsolately at the corners; even her clothes, though well cut and in the most ladylike if unfashionable taste, were of the same faded neutral tones. No, he did not like the pale personality and paler features of Valerie Pierson—but then he never had. Fond as he had always been of William Pierson, he had never been able to stand his wife—which was one of the main reasons he was now sitting guiltily riveted to his chair listening to her cultured, high-pitched, slightly nasal voice droning on; he had let his dislike of her stand in the way of old friendship, and this he knew was no way to behave.

"But how can you be sure he is missing at all?" he broke in. "He has been gone only three days. He may be off making a field survey or something."

"I've already *told* you it is just out of the question. To go off alone in the middle of an excavation *he* is directing without a word to anyone there! They haven't the faintest idea where he went, only that he took off with one of the

9

Jeeps and that's it. This Myron Goldsmith, his number-two man—a stooge for the Israelis if you ask me—" she added in a vicious aside, "*he* called me from Jerusalem because he thought Bill might have come back here."

"Why on earth should he think an extraordinary thing like that?" Toby demanded in astonishment. "Why should Bill fly back to England in the middle of the digging season?"

Her face closed up. "There's been a lot of trouble—personnel trouble, money, oh, all sorts of trouble. Bill has been under a lot of stress. Myron thought, well, he may have cracked under it—had to come home to think things out."

Toby's silvery eyebrows over his round blue eyes raised slightly. From what he had seen of the Piersons' marriage, which had had all the earmarks of a cold war, the thought of Bill flying back to the dubious comfort of his wife's charms was the very last one that would have occurred to him. In fact, the distressing idea came to him that if Bill were missing, it might well be a planned flight from an impossible domestic situation and a fading career . . . poor old Bill!

"Tell me more about this dig," he temporized. "I'm afraid I've been out of touch with what Bill has been doing, oh, ever since he left Africa. Must be all of five years, I'm sorry to say."

She looked vaguely impatient. "Oh, it's the excavation of an Essene monastery, a smaller version of the one at Qumran. It's still deeper into the Wilderness of Judea, between Ain Feshta and Engedi."

"Good heavens! What is he after, more Dead Sea scrolls?" Toby said facetiously and was surprised to see a hint of color rise in her pale cheeks.

"There is always that possibility," she said primly, but did not elaborate.

"I did not know anything that late or in that field was in Bill's line at all. What made him tackle a site like that?" he persisted.

She looked at him coldly. "After the debacle in Africa when we had to leave, Bill felt he needed a completely new field. He has been working with the commission studying the scroll scraps from Qumran up in Liverpool.

After all, it is not as if he were a complete stranger to the Middle East."

That was true enough, Toby thought gloomily, remembering another debacle Bill had been involved in early in his career. What rotten luck he had always had poor old Bill! Aloud he said, "I still feel you are overreacting to this. And, in any case, why come to me? There are so many people on the spot—his staff, the school in Jerusalem, the Israeli authorities—all much more capable of mounting a search for him than I am."

He was startled by her violent reaction. She leaned forward and almost hissed, "Because I need someone I can *trust,* and you've always claimed to be such a good friend of his. Besides, I know you are good at that sort of thing. I read all about the affair in Pergama, and your solving that crime in America from Italy. I *need* you. Why won't you help?"

Toby sighed inwardly and wished, not for the first time, that he had never launched himself into the choppy waters of detecting. "I'm afraid all those newspaper reports were grossly exaggerated," he muttered. "I played a very minor part in those affairs. My colleague, Dr. Spring, was the mainspring in both of them."

Valerie Pierson gave a derisive snort, then said, "Well, bring her, too, if she's so *necessary* to you, but come! I just know he has to be found, and quickly. It is the end of term and you have six whole weeks of vacation ahead of you; there is nothing to stop you from leaving tomorrow if you wished."

Toby's stubborn streak surged. Damn the woman! Calmly supposing that he had no other plans, nothing better to do than jump into action at her command. Well, he was double-damned if he was going to be badgered by this unpleasant female into abandoning his own comfortable projects to go rushing off to the wilderness to hunt for a man who, he was virtually sure, did not wish to be found. He got to his feet and straightened from his habitual scholar's stoop so that his tall, spindly frame towered over her. He wanted very much to end this uncomfortable tête-à-tête. "I am sorry," he said stiffly, "but I know Dr. Spring has her plans for the vacation, and so have I..I can't consider rushing off to Israel at a moment's notice. If you are as concerned as you seem to be, go to the Israeli authorities. If you like, I'll contact them for you myself."

She did not move from her chair but looked up at him with haunted, baffled eyes, her thin hands twisting nervously in her lap. For a moment she said nothing, then with great reluctance she whispered, "I dare not. I dare not go to the authorities. Sit down, Toby. I see I'll have to tell you everything. I did not want to; I didn't want to get you so involved, but I see I'll have to. . . . Bill is in a lot of trouble, a lot of danger, because actually he was doing something illegal. The excavation was just a cover for what he was really after . . ." She fumbled in her handbag and slipped a typewritten sheet across the desk toward him. "This is what he was doing—locating Zadok's treasure— and he wasn't going to let the Israelis have it!"

"Oh!" Toby said blankly and slumped back into his seat.

"He's had such rotten luck," she went on, appearing to go off on a tangent. "First in Iraq, then all the bickering and jealousy with Grayson that drove him from North Africa, then the East Africa business, which was no fault of his. No, he has never once had a break in all his career. This was to have been his one big stroke of luck—he was going to show you all finally what he could do . . ."

"But to go off on a wild-goose chase like this!" Toby spluttered. "When you say Zadok's treasure, I presume you mean the one mentioned in the Copper Scroll as being located near Zadok's tomb. I mean, most people think that the whole treasure business was a figment of some Zealot's imagination!"

"Not most people," she cut in, "just some people. There are a lot more who believe the Copper Scroll did contain true directions to the hidden treasure of the Temple of Jerusalem, which had been entrusted to the Essenes for hiding."

"But every time anyone has tried to use those directions, they have come up empty-handed," Toby protested. "This is nothing new. What could have possessed him to go off on the flimsy evidence of the scroll—it's just madness!"

A gleam of triumph came into the cold eyes and she leaned forward again. "That's just it—Bill had *more* information. I told you he had been working on those scraps of scrolls from Qumran 2—well, *one* of them contained the same information for the Zadok treasure as the Copper Scroll, *but there was more of it!* Enough so that Bill was certain he could find it. The locating of this new Essene monastery gave him just the additional bit of information he needed *and* the excuse to get out there."

"And who else knows about this?" Toby said weakly.

"No one; no one at all except me. There was no one he could trust with such a secret."

"But the other workers on the Liverpool project must know."

She colored faintly and shook her head. "They never saw that fragment. Oh, it's no use looking at me like that! It is all very well for you to be so Simon pure; you've had all the breaks. Bill was desperate, I tell you! When he saw what he had, he just took the fragment. He said nothing to anyone but me. But I am afraid someone out there may have been spying on him, don't you see? Maybe he has already located the treasure and they have done something to him to get it . . . oh, I don't know!" Her voice rose querulously. "But I've *got* to find out what has happened to him. Please help me!"

"Well, that certainly does alter things," Toby said and pulled the typewritten sheet toward him.

In the cistern, which is below the rampart on the east side in a place hollowed out of the rock, there will be found 600 large bars of silver. Close by under the southern corner of Zadok's tomb and underneath a column of pilaster in the excedras, there is a golden incense vessel of pine wood and another of cassia. In the pit nearby toward the north and near to the grave in a hole opening to the north, there is a copy of this book with explanations, measurements and all details for the rest.

It was just a translation of part of the Copper Scroll and familiar to Toby, but he studied it with minute attention to cover the whirling confusion of his thoughts. What if Bill had already found what he was after and had taken off; what if this waspish woman in front of him had only known part of the plan? There had been plenty of

rumors that Bill had an eye for the ladies, and small wonder! But, on the other hand, what if he was really in trouble somewhere out there in the stark desert of Judea? What
the hell ought he to do? To gain more time he asked,
"Just supposing Bill has located the site and is working on
it—wouldn't that account for his absence?"

She shook her head impatiently. "No, that wasn't the
plan. Once he had located it, he was going to close down
the dig as soon as possible, and we were to go after it
alone. Also, the arrangement was that he would use a code
phrase that we had worked out before he left when he'd
phone me. He would drive up to Jerusalem once a week
for supplies and do that, and the last time there was nothing—in fact, he sounded very disheartened."

"Then perhaps I ought to take a look," Toby said with
extreme reluctance.

"Oh, yes, *yes*," she said feverishly. "I'm leaving tomorrow on the noon flight. I got an extra ticket just in case . . ."

A small panic seized Toby. "You're coming?"

"Well of course I am, he's my husband," she snapped.
"Of course I'm coming with you."

"I shall have to have a completely free hand to operate,"
Toby spluttered. "I'm afraid I just couldn't do so with you
on the site, particularly if there is trouble out there. If I
come, I would have to insist you stay in Jerusalem until
I come up with something definite. You could, perhaps,
assist Dr. Spring with investigations there."

"She's coming?" It was her turn to be startled.

"Well I'll have to check," Toby said hastily, "but she
really is very necessary, if I am to look into this on a
confidential basis."

"You mean you would not do it without her?"

"No!" Toby almost exploded. "Out of the question!"
And he hoped fervently that Penny would be reasonable;
she would just have to keep this damned woman away from
him.

"I had not bargained on that much expense," Valerie
said reluctantly.

Toby's heart hardened. Valerie Pierson was a rich
woman; one of the reasons—the *main* reason, he had always suspected—that Bill had married her, but she also
had the reputation of a penny-pincher. Well, this time she

wasn't going to get away with it! "I will take care of my own expenses," he said coldly, "but I must insist if you want me to come that you cover Dr. Spring's expenses, since, unlike you and me, she has no inherited wealth to draw on."

"Oh, very well!" she said, vexedly. "But how soon can you leave?"

"I don't know. I shall have to ask her. It may be impossible." He shambled to his feet and edged out of his barricade. "Wait here; I'll have to find Dr. Spring and see what her plans are."

Once outside the office, he let out an explosive sigh. Hell's teeth! What had he got himself into! He went up the short flight of steps to Penny's office just above his own and tapped on the door. Without waiting for a reply, he stuck his silver-thatched, knoblike head around the door. "You busy?" he demanded.

Penny was seated behind her desk, her short, mouse-colored hair standing up in spikes, her little monkeylike face screwed up in an agony of concentration as a large red pencil hovered in her hand above a pile of papers on the desk in front of her. She looked over the top of her reading glasses at him as he slipped into the room and said, "Yes I am—very. A bunch of finals to correct—one of the most addlepated classes I've had in a long time. So, good bye, Toby; see you later. Lunch—okay?"

"Wait!" he said hastily. "This is terribly important, Penny, or I wouldn't bother you. I need your help. What are your plans for the Easter vacation?"

"Is that all? I told you last week. For the last two weeks of it, I'm going to the U.S.—(a) to see Alex in Baltimore, and (b) to attend Alexander Dimola's wedding in New York. Remember I told you about that? Just as I predicted, he is marrying a steel tycoon's daughter—much more suitable than the last one—and they are having a terrific shindig for the wedding . . ."

"But before that," he managed to break in.

"Well, I planned to paint the cottage. It needs it. I planned to do it last year but never had time with all that to-do on Cape Cod."

"Would you consider coming to Israel with me?"

"Israel!" She brightened. "What on earth for?"

"It's a case," he tempted.

"Murder?" She brightened even more.

"No, or at least I certainly hope not. A disappearance—Bill Pierson, we stayed with him once briefly out in East Africa. Remember?"

She pondered. "Oh, yes, a nice little man, but a frightful wife, as I recall. He's vanished?"

"Yes. His wife is very worried—he may be in serious trouble. . . . Rapidly Toby sketched out the background.

"Whew! Manhunting and treasure-hunting in the Palestinian desert, eh? Sounds much more to my taste than painting the cottage," Penny said happily. "When do we start?"

"Well, Valerie Pierson is flying out tomorrow. We'll leave then, if possible. And—er—my idea was that I should go down to the dig and you could—er—backstop me in Jerusalem. With all the trouble on the West Bank, I'd not want you to take the risk of coming down there with me."

Penny looked at him in silence for a moment, her hazel eyes shrewd. "Why, you cunning old so-and-so," she said at last, jumping immediately to the right conclusion, "you want me along to ride herd on that ghastly woman, don't you, not to help investigate at all. Of all the nerve! I've a good mind to say no."

"No, it's not that at all," Toby lied desperately. "There's lots you can do to help me in Jerusalem, and I won't get anywhere with her dogging my footsteps. *Please*, Penny—I need you!"

There was a twinkle in her eye as she stared him down. "Hmm," she said at last, "I suppose turnabout is fair play. I ruined your last spring vacation on behalf of an old friend, so I suppose the least I can do in return is a favor on behalf of an old friend of yours. Besides, you're always wailing about how I'm constantly getting into hot water. This time the shoe seems to be on the other foot. I'd better come along to see you don't get in too deep. But I'll come with one proviso—I take off for America on schedule no matter what happens. Okay?"

Toby gave a relieved sigh. "Oh, fine, just fine. It should not take more than a week or two at most."

"Don't tempt fate!" Penny snapped with a little shiver. "This may not be as simple as you think. Sometimes your confidence in your own powers frightens me. Life occasionally does pull the rug out from under you, you know."

Toby ignored her admonition. "So I'll tell her yes? When shall I say we'll go?"

"Why not tomorrow noon?" Penny said, picking up her red pencil again. "As soon as I've finished these, I'll go home and throw a few things in a bag and that's that. How about you?"

"Oh, I'll be there on time."

But when he returned to his office, it was to find his visitor gone. A note in tiny, cramped handwriting stood propped against his tobacco jar.

Having so many last-minute things to take care of, I can wait no longer, but will meet you at the Heathrow terminal at the British Airways checkin counter at 11 A.M. tomorrow. Kindly tell no one else about your trip.

Sincerely,
Valerie Pierson

Underneath was an airplane ticket to Tel Aviv.

"The nerve of her!" Toby muttered. "That insufferable woman! What have I got myself into? Poor old Bill!"

CHAPTER 2

Persons abroad early the next day at the railway station in the fair city of Oxford were treated to an unusual spectacle—the tall figure of the distinguished professor of archaeology, Sir Tobias Glendower, and the short, dumpy figure of the equally distinguished Mathieson Reader in anthropology, Dr. Penelope Spring, flanked by two running porters, making a highly undignified scramble for the early-morning London express.

"Did you have to bring so much stuff?" Toby puffed as he attempted to wrestle two large suitcases onto the luggage rack of their first-class compartment while the train clattered into motion. Penny, panting like a wheezy Pekingese, glared glazedly at the Oxford gasworks sliding out of sight but said nothing.

"You'll be pounds overweight," he continued in an aggrieved tone as he settled into a corner opposite her and started to fill his pipe. "We're not *emigrating* to Israel, you know."

Penny continued to pant but pointed mutely to the No Smoking sign on the window. "Well, there's no one here but us," Toby continued his soliloquy as he emitted his first cloud of blue smoke, "and *you* don't mind."

Penny gulped and finally got her voice back into working condition. "To go back to the remark before last," she wheezed, "I forgot to ask you yesterday what the climate would be like this time of year, and your phone was busy all evening, so I came prepared for all contingencies. The only time I was in Israel before was on a bus tour one January, and it was *cold*."

Toby shuddered delicately, the shudder being directed at the thought of the bus tours rather than the climate; he had never adjusted to Penny's propensity for haring off to all parts of the globe on the proverbial shoestring. "Well, it should be very pleasant just now," he averred. "Like England in July—a *good* July," he amended.

"Oh, in that case I'll do a repack at the airport if we have time," Penny said cheerfully. "I can always leave one of the cases at the left-luggage area. Incidentally, are we meeting Valerie Pierson there? Is she coming on the same flight?"

"Yes, I got in touch with her last night," Toby said and frowned. "Extraordinary woman, rushing off like that! Went back to her London apartment as calm as you please, assuming as a matter of course we'd fall in with her plans. Some nerve!"

"Then I suggest we put this train journey to good use," Penny said as she settled back into her seat. "If we're going to be stuck with her from now on, we won't have much of an opportunity to talk privately, and if I am to be of any help at all I need to be filled in on everything you know about Bill and Valerie Pierson *and* the set-up we are going into. I mean, I don't intend just sitting around playing watchdog on her all the time, that's for sure."

"She may be more of a handful than you think," Toby warned. "But I see your point. What do you want to know?"

"Everything. Assume I've never heard of either of them. Start from when you first knew him."

Toby's round blue eyes behind their equally round glasses grew reflective. "That goes back quite a way. Bill was at my college, you know, but a year behind me. We were thrown together a lot because we were the only two in the archaeological field—but there all resemblance ended. Everything was so hard for Bill; he had no money, he was up on a state scholarship—in fact, had gone through state grammar schools on scholarships. His father was a factory worker up north somewhere and there was a large family. Anyway, you know what a snobbish college Magdalen was back then. He had a very hard time. I always felt so sorry for him . . ." Toby trailed off into silence for a moment, and Penny looked at him with knowing hazel eyes. Poor Toby; his father's riches had always aroused guilt feelings in him, for which no amount of his own accomplishments had ever been able to compensate. "But, by God, how Bill worked!" he went on. "A lot of it came terribly hard to him, but he stuck with it, oh, fourteen or fifteen hours a day. He managed to wangle another postgraduate grant to see him through a B.Litt., and had all sorts of trouble getting that. Always seemed to have difficulty seeing the forest for the trees . . ."

"Meaning he didn't have any talent," Penny put in bluntly.

"No, I wouldn't say *that*." Toby looked pained. "It was just that he'd labor very hard to produce something that, well, did not amount to a great deal. It was the same when he started excavating on his own. Draper of London once put it in a nutshell when he said that Bill always found nothing, but he found it in the neatest and cleanest possible way. I suppose he just lacked the golden touch that great archaeologists like Woolley or Wheeler or Mellaart have had."

"And you," Penny added to herself.

". . . so after he finally got through Oxford, he went out to Iraq on one of those long-term Anglo-American digs. Only unfortunately it did not turn out to be so long-term. I never knew the whole story behind it, but after three seasons the Iraqi government closed it down and threw them all out. It was there he first crossed swords with Selwyn Grayson—one of those feuds that seem to get started so easily in this field. I suppose it was the old story: both young and with the same interests and with a name to make, both highly competitive. And the hard time Bill had had did make him a bit dogmatic at times. He came back to England out of a job, but it was about this time he met up with Valerie and married her very quickly. I think he felt he finally had a lucky break, because she was an heiress—a jam fortune, I think it was, or possibly chocolate—anyway, while the marriage undoubtedly helped him in one sense, I believe in the long run it hindered him. She has always used the money to club him down, and while Bill has always had a certain amount of trouble relating to people, *she* can't relate to anyone at all, and that has been a terrible drag on him over the years. She staked him to several digs in North Africa, but there he ran up against Selwyn Grayson again; the old feud flared, and when it came to the plum job as director of antiquities for Algeria, Bill lost out to him. The Piersons retreated to

East Africa, and you remember what pomp and circumstance she kept when we visited them there. He did well enough with his digging, but then came a military coup and they got booted out with all the other 'rich foreigners,' and so he was out in the cold once more. He just has had the worst luck!"

"Sounds like a born loser to me," Penny said firmly. "I must say I feel a sneaking sympathy with Valerie. It can't be much fun to be hitched to a man who is always on the losing end of the stick. If I were Mrs. Moneybags, I think I'd have been tempted to ditch him long ago—particularly if, as you say, he has always had a roving eye."

"Those are just rumors," Toby said uncomfortably. "I don't know anything definite. And I think you'll find your sympathy with Valerie will rapidly disappear on closer acquaintance. She has made Bill pay in sweat and tears for every penny she has ever given him. It is what I am most afraid of now; if he really has got onto something in the treasure line, I think he may well be so desperate that he'll just scoot with it as far and as fast as he can—a very messy situation indeed."

"That remains to be seen," Penny said reprovingly. "So what is the set-up at the excavation?"

"From our telephone conversation last night, I gather it is quite a small-scale affair." Toby got out his notebook and consulted it. "There's Myron Goldsmith, who is a London University lecturer and the assistant director; Ali-Muhammed, who was Bill's sidekick in the old Iraqi days; a couple of students who are paying their own way for the experience—Hedecai Schmidt, a young Israeli architecture student, and an American, Robert Dyke . . ."

"Robert Dyke," Penny echoed. "That name sounds familiar! Where on earth have I heard it? Not too long ago, either."

Toby shrugged his shoulders and went on. "Then there's John Carter, a British Foreign Office type who was a friend of theirs in East Africa—apparently an amateur archaeology buff; and Tahir, a Kurdish foreman—I knew someone in Turkey called that, but it couldn't be the same one—and about a half-dozen Arab workmen. That's it."

"They don't sound a very sinister bunch," Penny commented.

"No, but rather an ill-assorted one. According to Valerie, Myron Goldsmith and Ali-Muhammed have been at daggers from the word go, and Tahir the foreman, who controls the diggers, does not get on with either one, so the digging has been going along at a snail's pace. . . ." Toby sighed heavily. "I'm really not relishing the idea of going into this hotbed. I only hope this Carter fellow is a reasonable chap and I can get some help from him. Valerie seems to think he is the only trustworthy one of the whole bunch."

"And she is footing the bill for it all?"

"Not entirely. London University kicked in some money, which is why Myron Goldsmith is along, I gather, and the British School in Jerusalem gave them a small grant, but even so, it's a shoestring operation. They are living in tents on the site and were only planning a six-week dig, almost three of which have already gone by with virtually no results."

"So what is our plan of action?" Penny unwrapped a chocolate bar and gave it a thoughtful munch.

Toby turned a stern blue eye on her. *"Yours* is to keep Valerie busy in Jerusalem. I'll go down to the site, see what's what there and mount a search for Bill. In spite of what Valerie says, I am certain someone there must have some idea where he went."

"And if you come up empty-handed?"

"I'll go to the Israeli authorities. I don't care if that does upset Valerie or the apple cart. If Bill *is* in trouble out there, this is no time for amateurs. The Wilderness of Judea is no place to mess around with; we'll have to find him fast. I only hope it's not too late already," he added gloomily.

Penny finished her snack and started to burrow into her tote bag again, emerging with a crumpled handful of exam papers and her red pencil. "Didn't quite finish and must get them done before London," she explained, settling back into her seat, "but one final thought: it strikes me that if things are as bad between the Piersons as you say, and if those rumors about him being a ladies' man are true, it might be worthwhile to *cherchez la femme.* Since there is only one girl on the dig and she is still there, it does not sound as if she's a likely candidate, but it may be worth my having a look-see around Jerusalem for one. Any ideas on where I might start looking or where his tastes lie?"

Toby cogitated. "In his student days he liked them blonde and nubile, but who knows? I'm sure I don't. As to where —well, again, it's anyone's guess. This is his first venture in Israel and he hasn't been out there all that often or that long. The British School, the Department of Antiquities, the hotel where the staff stayed for the few days it took to set the dig up, the airport—none of them very likely in my opinion, but it may be worth a try."

Another thought occurred to Penny. "Is Bill a publicity hound? I mean, that is a possibility if the dig wasn't working out, if the treasure hunt was a bust. To disappear might at least get him some notice."

"No. I'd say out of the question. Bill has had so many unfortunate experiences with journalists that that would be the last way he'd go. Besides, if he were still after the treasure, it would be quite insane."

"Oh, yes, that's the other thing I meant to ask you about. Tell me more about that. You don't believe in it—why not?"

Toby cleared his throat and went into his lecturing rumble. "Because according to the Copper Scroll, the treasure consists of twenty-six tons of gold and sixty-five tons of silver, besides other valuables, all hidden in some sixty-odd different caches around the country. The thought that the Essenes, who were pledged to simple living, could have amassed such a treasure themselves is ridiculous, so some scholars have thought it was the Jerusalem Temple's treasure entrusted to their safekeeping. But when you think of the history of the Temple, it does not make too much sense. We *know* it was completely looted by the Assyrians and then by the Babylonians. True, it was restored under the Maccabees, but that gives a bare two hundred years before the *Roman* destruction of the Temple for them to have built up such a treasure, during which time Israel was never in a good political position, made no foreign conquests, and, in short, was in no shape to amass so much. I might be persuaded to believe in a tenth of it, but not as stated in the Copper Scroll."

"But in that case what would be the purpose of writing the scroll?" Penny said practically. "Wasn't it deliberately hidden for later generations, and wasn't the fact that it was etched in copper rather than written on the normal skin scroll indicative that it *was* terribly important and had to be indestructible?"

Toby sighed and shrugged. "You have just used two of the main reasons advanced by the 'treasure-believers,' and I can't answer you. I don't know why a Zealot would do such a thing. The motive is totally obscure. All I can say is that based on the *earlier,* undoubted historical evidence, it just does not make any kind of sense."

"Twenty-six tons of gold," Penny murmured thoughtfully. "With gold at the price it is, doesn't that represent a fantastic amount?"

"The gold alone would be worth more than one hundred and eighty-six *million* dollars," Toby volunteered. "High stakes indeed!"

"I'll say! If I were the Israeli government, I would have the whole army complete with metal detectors out after it. Even if they didn't believe in it, it would be worth a try."

"The fact that they haven't done any such thing shows they don't believe in it any more than I do," Toby said mildly.

"And you say Bill had some additional information that made him go after one specific treasure hoard. What was so special about that one?"

"Because Zadok is a known historical figure—high priest to Solomon and the founder of a long line of Temple high priests. In spite of all the ups and downs Israel had after his time, the memory of his tomb was green up to and beyond the Roman destruction. It is mentioned in several places besides the Copper Scroll and remains one of the few places—granting all the destruction and physical changes that have gone on in Palestine since then—that may feasibly be relocated. You've seen the directions—what did you make of them?"

Penny frowned in thought. "Well, all this business about cisterns and excedras and pillars certainly sounds like a built-up place, not at all what you would expect to find in the wilderness. And surely the high priest would *not* be buried out in the desert like that. I mean, if he were a VIP, wouldn't he be planted somewhere visible? And I must say, compared to the figures you quoted for the rest, this treasure does not amount to much—only one gold vessel and the rest in silver bars."

"Exactly right so far as the location goes"—Toby nodded indulgently as if to a bright student—"but you have missed the whole point of this particular treasure. The most precious thing in it is the book the scribe mentions with such great precision."

"But that was just another copy of the Copper Scroll," Penny protested.

Toby shook his head. *"No!* Think about it—what sense would it make to have just another copy? We know the Copper Scroll itself was written in haste during the last days of the Zealots' stand against the Romans, and that it was placed in the Qumran cave years after the rest of the scrolls found there. The chances are that if the treasure did exist, even in part, it had been hidden at the very beginning of the rebellion, when hopes were still high for success, and that *exact* directions to its refinding were recorded in a normal scroll. Find that scroll and you probably could locate the rest of the treasure!"

"Wow!" Penny said in awe. "So it would be the archaeological find of all time. No wonder Valerie Pierson is so worried!"

"Yes, and one would not have to be an archaeologist to be willing to cut a few throats for a stake that high," Toby pointed out grimly.

The train clattered over some points, and Penny glanced out the window. "Slough already!" she exclaimed in dismay. "I just have to get these papers done before we get to Paddington, so do bé quiet, Toby."

Looking pained, he retreated behind a cloud of blue smoke and a copy of the London *Times* until the train clanked into the echoing confines of the station.

As they wrestled the bags down from the rack and looked vainly for a porter, Penny suddenly exclaimed, "Now I remember where I heard that name before! But it couldn't possibly be the same one."

"What name?"

"Robert Dyke, of course! He was the young man who found the body in the bog on Cape Cod. I saw him at the inquest. You don't suppose . . . ? No, much too fantastic. . . ."

Toby hefted two of the heavy suitcases and proceeded to trudge up the platform. "Well, if he is the same one, I certainly hope he does not make a habit of it," he said grumpily. "We've got enough trouble as it is."

CHAPTER 3

They arrived at Heathrow early and in time to witness a curious little incident. They dealt with the baggage and had moved up to the departure lounge, where Penny was still scribbling away on her exam papers and Toby reflectively puffing on his pipe beside her, when he exclaimed, "There she is now!" Penny looked up to see the tall, thin figure of Valerie, head bent and deep in conversation with a small fat man, whose dark suit, bowler hat, furled umbrella and black leather briefcase screamed of "someone in the City." Oblivious to the fact that they were being watched, the pair sat down on a leather bench close by and continued the heated exchange. The little man opened his briefcase and gesticulated with a thick sheaf of papers in his hand. "I suppose I'd better let her know we're here," Toby said reluctantly and got up.

Penny, who had been watching the little tableau with bright-eyed curiosity, hastily stowed her own papers away. "I'll come with you."

They were right next to the engrossed couple before Toby rumbled, "Hello, Valerie. We are all set for the flight. How about you? Everything all right?"

Valerie looked up and shrank back, twin spots of color flaring in her pallid cheeks, and gasped, "What are you doing here so soon!" The man looked equally startled, the sheaf of papers in his fat little hand poised in mid-air. Penny, who was an expert at reading things upside down, read their superscription and her eyebrows rose a notch.

Toby was looking at Valerie in amazement. "We are getting the same plane as you, are we not? We came down by the early train."

With a visible effort Valerie pulled herself together. "Oh, of course! I just did not expect to see you this early. This is Mr. Doyle, er, one of my legal advisors—Sir Tobias Glendower, Dr. Spring. They are accompanying me to

Israel." The little man shot her a curious glance, opened his mouth to say something, closed it again, shoveled the papers back into his bag and muttered, "How d'you do." He stood up. "I must be going. You *will* let me know how things progress, Mrs. Pierson, won't you?"

Valerie was once more in complete control of herself. She nodded at him coldly and said again, "Of course, as soon as possible." He gave a stiff little bow and scurried off, leaving the ill-assorted trio gazing after him in silence.

Toby broke it, glancing at his watch. "How about a drink? We have a few minutes before boarding and we should discuss ongoing arrangements. I don't suppose you will wish to join us in the smoking section, Valerie?" His tone was hopeful.

"No, indeed!" She looked with distaste at his pipe. "But perhaps a drink would be a good idea. I do so detest long journeys."

Seated over the drinks, she deigned to address Penny for the first time. "I'm afraid I have done nothing about your hotel arrangements, Dr. Spring. In the first place I was not sure you would insist on coming, and in the second I did not know what travel arrangements you usually have with Toby—one room or two."

Penny took a quick look at Toby, who was silently swelling and turning purple in the face, kicked him smartly on the ankle to avert the coming explosion and said sweetly, "Oh, two—always two—Toby snores so. And I am sure anywhere you have elected to stay will be good enough for me. I'm not at all fussy. Where is that, by the way?"

"The Sheikh Jarrah Hotel," Valerie snapped. "It is in the Sheikh Jarrah quarter of Jerusalem, close by the Jericho Road. It is where my husband stayed."

"Well, just so long as it is clean," Penny murmured. "Also I am a little bit puzzled. I had gathered you had engaged my professional services, Mrs. Pierson."

"What professional services?"

"As an investigator," Penny continued blandly, "as a professional investigator. Didn't Toby make that clear?" She looked reproachfully at his still-apoplectic countenance.

"But you're an anthropologist!" Valerie spluttered.

"Oh, just part-time," Penny said with a perfectly straight face. "I'm also a part-time investigator. For my last case I received five thousand dollars, but since you are a friend of Toby's, I would not dream of charging you that much. Say just thirty dollars a day and expenses?"

"But . . . but . . . that's preposterous! I had no idea when Toby said he had to have you along . . . I naturally assumed . . ." Valerie stammered.

"Oh, dear! Well, if this is not agreeable to you, I'm afraid I shall have to withdraw," Penny went on, at which point Toby finally got his voice back and joined in the game.

"In that case, of course, I could not proceed either," he added.

Valerie looked from one to the other in stunned disbelief and faltered, "No—no—that's all right. You must come. I'll manage it somehow." She was so visibly shaken that she lapsed into silence until the boarding announcement blared from the PA system.

When they were airborne, Toby gave vent to his pent-up feelings. "What did I tell you! That insufferable woman! Of all the nerve!"

Penny looked up from the Israel tour guide she was busily leafing through with an amused grin. "I thought I settled her hash rather well myself." Her brow furrowed. "But you know there is more to our pallid Valerie than meets the eye, and there are one or two things I just don't understand. You say she is loaded?"

"Yes, well, so I have always understood."

"Then just look at this." She handed him the guidebook. "The Sheikh Jarrah is only a two-star hotel. Not that there is anything against that, but you would think if she's that rich she'd stay at one of the posher places like the Jerusalem Hilton or the Intercontinental."

"But she said Bill had stayed at that one. He has always had simple tastes, and it makes a lot of sense to go to the same one."

"I suppose so. But look how taken aback she was when I indicated I expected to be paid."

"I told you she was tightfisted."

"And another thing: she has a rather curious definition of a legal advisor. Little Mr. Doyle was an insurance man."

Toby looked at her popeyed. "How do you know that?"

"Because it was stamped on the papers he was holding. 'Edward Doyle, Liberty Life Insurance Company.' And the papers, incidentally, were a life insurance policy on Bill Pierson; *his* name was on them too. Curious, isn't it? I am sure Valerie wants you to find her husband, but I am really beginning to wonder if she wants you to find him alive or *dead!*"

Myron Goldsmith made his way wearily back to his tent at the end of another horrendous and generally fruitless working day. The shadows were lengthening like stark black fingers reaching out from the cliffs above, barring the small plateau on which the camp stood; but beyond, where the ground fell sharply away to the plain in empty, barren gullies, the sun still shone, striking blinding reflections from the empty, sinister waters of the Dead Sea. He threw a hopeless, haggard glance around the little camp, which was settling into the pattern of its evening activities, and then, entering the tent, he flopped down on the narrow camp cot and got out a bottle of gin from the tin footlocker under it. He sighed and took a large swig of the burning liquid. He shuddered and choked, but its fire had an immediate effect on the racking tenseness in him. He relaxed back onto the cot, sighed again and felt, as he had felt for the past month, that he was a man much put upon.

How the hell had he ever got into this mess? How the hell was he ever going to explain all this to London University? What the devil was he to do? Nothing had gone right from the very start, nothing, and now this . . . ! He took another long swig and shuddered again.

It had been bad enough with Bill Pierson here, but now, four days after he had taken off in the Jeep for God knows where, things were worse, much worse.

No one appeared to take any notice of what he said. Every time he turned his back someone else had gone off without a word; it was bad enough when John Carter did it, but at least he was a free agent; but when Ali-Muhammed, who after all was *paid* to be here, took a leaf out of his employer's book and went off too, it really was the limit!

Everybody was against him, Myron thought bleakly. Even those two damn students always had their heads together, laughing at him most probably, and disappearing as soon as he took his eyes off them. And that surly bastard of a foreman! Trying to tell *him* how things should be run. And on top of all this, the latest arrival, whose coming he knew could bode no good. He could see the headlines now. DESERT FIASCO OF BRITISH ARCHAEOLOGICAL TEAM. He would be ruined, a laughingstock. He wished now he had never put in that call to Mrs. Pierson. He should have gone straight to the Israeli authorities and let the chips fall where they might. The damned woman was probably on her way out right now, and what was he to tell her?

The sound of a car engine cut into his thoughts and brought him unsteadily to his feet. Dear God, that surely could not be her already!

Peering out of the tent flap through misted glasses, he could see a Jeep laboring up the steep incline to the camp from the track below. His first feeling was relief, for although he could not make out who was driving it, whoever it was was wearing a very yellowed and battered Panama hat with a narrow black ribbon the like of which he had not seen outside of old Charlie Chan movies. Obviously it was not Mrs. Pierson.

The Jeep reached the little plateau and ground to a shuddering halt, and Myron's eyes widened as he recognized the figure who was slowly uncoiling from the driver's seat as one he had last seen gracing the podium of the Society of Antiquaries at Burlington House. "Good God, what's *he* doing here," Myron muttered to himself, and was about to step out to take this new situation in hand when the evening peace of the camp was shattered by a stentorian bellow.

"Glendower-*effendi!* It is you! *Hos geldiniz! Nasilsiniz?*" White pantaloons flapping, his shabby blue jacket flying with his sheer momentum, the great burly figure of Tahir the foreman hurled itself toward the tall, thin man by the Jeep, who was now peering somewhat myopically through his round glasses, a fixed expression of anxious surprise on his equally round face, which was like that of an elderly baby. Tahir, who topped Toby's six feet by at least four inches, engulfed the frailer man in a bearlike hug. "Glendower-*Bey,* I had never thought to see thee more in this world. Truly you are a gift from Allah! Now all will be well."

"Tahir! It really *is* you! I did not think it possible."
Toby disentangled himself and peered into the grinning,
bearded brigand's face of the big Kurd. He slipped through
a time tunnel of thirty years when, as a stripling student,
he had thought the Kurd already old. Yet here he was
unchánged, unmarked by time, while he himself . . . An ex-
quisite feeling of relief swept over him; here at least was
one ally he could count on, and, what was more, an ally
who could supply him with one of the tools he needed
most—the language!

Toby's grasp of languages was remarkable. He could
speak a dozen fluently and understood a half-dozen more,
but Hebrew and Arabic for some strange reason had always eluded him, and this fact had been worrying him all
the way from England. He grinned and slapped the big
man affectionately on the shoulder. "Why, you old ruffian,"
he said in Turkish, "I thought you had been gathered to
Allah's bosom long since, and yet here you are as strong
and as frisky as ever! I am more happy to see you than you
can believe. I have great need of you."

The Kurd gave another great bellow of laughter. "The
great Glendower-*bey* needs me! Y'Allah, that is something
indeed! My hands are your hands, my strength is your
strength. Together we will move the mountain to Muham-
mad, eh?"

Toby became aware of a small, wiry figure advancing
on them somewhat unsteadily; a white-faced, dark-haired,
youngish man, the dominant feature of his face being
tinted, strong, bifocal glasses which masked the eyes and
gave him the look of a pallid beetle. "Sir Tobias Glendower?" he asked hesitantly. "I'm Myron Goldsmith, in-
terim director of the dig. Er—this is something of a surprise. I had no idea you were coming. Er, what can I do
for you?"

Tahir muttered something under his breath that Toby did
not catch and stamped off, while he took Goldsmith's prof-
fered hand and shook it gingerly; it was both sweaty and
cold.

"I've come to find Bill Pierson," Toby said simply.
"Mrs. Pierson felt it was a matter of some urgency and
speed was of the essence, so here I am."

"You're *staying* here!" Myron Goldsmith seemed completely dumbfounded.

"Why, yes. I gather Bill *isn't* back, so I stay until either he turns up or I find him." Toby's gaze took in the collection of drab green tents and lingered curiously on a bright orange one that was set up a little apart from the others and had a brand-new Land Rover parked beside it.

"Er, we're not really set up for visitors," Myron said apologetically.

Toby turned a cold blue gaze on him. "I've brought my own supplies, and I thought I could bunk down in Bill's tent for the moment. If you'll show me to it, I'll get my gear unloaded, and then I would like to hear what you have been doing to find him."

Myron recoiled. "Well, er, of course. This way." But there was yet another interruption. The flap of the bright orange tent opened and a tall, red-haired figure emerged, stood rigid for a second and then came loping toward them. "Good to see you again, Glendower," it called in a high, nasal voice. "Come to see Bill's latest foul-up? Boy! When you get a gander at this one, you'll see it's a chestnut that even you couldn't pull out of the fire."

Toby heard Myron Goldsmith suck in his breath sharply beside him and tried to conceal his own surprise. Selwyn Grayson came up to them and stood with his hands on his hips, a smirk on his hatchetlike face.

"I had no idea you were part of this expedition, Dr. Grayson," Toby said stiffly.

Selwyn held up his hands in mock horror. "Perish the thought! Just dropped by a couple of days ago to see what Bill was up to. Touring, y'know, to see how the other half lives." His contemptuous gaze swept over the camp and came back to rest on Goldsmith. "And what do I find but Bill cavorting off somewhere and poor old Myron left here holding the bag. Maybe you can stay and help the poor boy out." The sneer was unmistakable. "I think it's all too much for him. Can I give you a hand with your gear?"

"No, thanks," Toby said shortly. He looked over at Tahir, who had reappeared and was hovering on the outskirts of the group glowering at Grayson. "Take my stuff to Pierson-*bey*'s tent, will you?" he said in Turkish.

"*Evet, effendi,*" Tahir said and leaped into action.

Grayson's eyes narrowed. "You two know each other? And what's that lingo?"

"Turkish," Toby said blandly. "And Tahir and I are old friends."

This piece of news seemed to disconcert Grayson markedly, because he backed off and said, "Well, see you later then," and hurried back to his tent.

Toby cocked an eyebrow at Myron Goldsmith, who was now sweating visibly. "What in the name of heaven is *he* doing here?"

Myron gave a hopeless shrug. "I haven't the faintest idea. He just showed up out of the blue almost three days ago. Said he had to see Bill and has been hanging around ever since, doing his damnedest to make things worse than they are already."

"And how long was that after Bill took off exactly?"

"Oh, just about thirty-six hours." Myron's tone was wretched with worry. "The trouble is we don't know exactly when Bill left, only that it was sometime during the day. The dig is about five hundred yards from here, just around that spur out of sight of the camp, and we were all busy there. He apparently told one of the students to fetch something for him from the site, and that was the last time he was seen. When we came back to camp that night, one of the Jeeps was gone, so we assumed he'd taken off in that."

"Had he taken any camping equipment or supplies with him?" Toby tried not to sound too concerned.

Myron shrugged again. "I don't know. I don't know what he had with him. Nothing appears to be gone from his tent. As to the supplies, well, with the damn Arabs filching so much stuff, it is hard to tell. The man who does the cooking is always complaining about running out of something or another."

Toby's eyebrows rose a little further. This was something he would obviously have to go into with Tahir. "I just thought he'd gone off to Jerusalem," Myron went on. "Then when he didn't come back . . ." He trailed off and shook his head.

"Later on I'd like to get all this down," Toby said firmly, "but for now I'd like to wash up after that dusty ride. Then I'd like to meet the other members of the expedition."

Myron looked at his watch. "It'll be dinnertime soon; you can meet them all then. But while we are alone, there is one question I would like to ask you, sir." He hesitated.

"Yes?" Toby prompted.

"If Mrs. Pierson is so concerned about her husband's absence, why hasn't she gone to the Israeli authorities? She gave no indication to me when I talked to her that she was so upset, but if she is, surely they are the people to call in. I mean, why drag you all the way out here?"

Toby took the time to light his pipe and made sure it was drawing properly before answering. "I am one of Bill's oldest friends," he said carefully, "so it was quite natural for Mrs. Pierson to come to me. Although she is concerned about his unexplained absence, she is equally concerned not to involve the Israeli authorities in what may only be a false alarm, and which could possibly result in unfortunate publicity for the expedition. I'm sure you can appreciate that." He gazed levelly at the younger man, who dropped his eyes and muttered, "Yes, but it has left me in a very difficult position."

"I realize that, and I assure you that if, in the next day or so, I do not come up with an explanation for Bill's absence, I am going to the Israeli authorities myself." Toby was definite.

But for some reason this statement, far from comforting him, seemed to cast Myron into even deeper gloom as he led the way toward Bill Pierson's abandoned tent.

Seated later in the mess tent, Toby helped himself to a stiff shot of Scotch from the bottle he had thoughtfully brought with him and looked down the long trestle table covered with a drab-colored plastic cloth. Outside a night wind had sprung up off the Dead Sea and was keening in the darkness. It was chilly, and Toby was grateful for the warmth of the old sports jacket he had brought with him.

The faces about the table were all unfamiliar to him, but the scene itself was all too familiar. The harsh glare of the two Coleman lamps sitting on the table made the mess tent a place of violent light and shadow without nuances, picked dull gleams from the piled bowl of Jaffa oranges on the table, the stainless-steel cutlery, the coarse tumblers and the bottles arrayed by each person's place, each with its

careful pencil mark to mitigate the endless petty dis-
putes that were part and parcel of the rough life of an
archaeological camp. His canvas camp chair ground grit-
tily on the dry earth of the tent floor. Over everything
there hung the film and the smell of desert earth, which,
mixing with the hot smell of the hissing lamps, reminded
him of the dozens of times he had sat in similar surroundings, with the same mixture of excited anticipation for the
morrow and physical weariness for the day.

But this was not his dig; this was Bill's. He was sitting
in Bill's place, looking at Bill's staff; he must see them
through Bill's eyes. He looked at the bottles on the table.
You could tell a lot about a person by what he drank, he
thought. Goldsmith, at the opposite end of the table from
him, was a gin drinker and, by the rapidity with which
the level in the bottle in front of him was going down, a
heavy one at that. The fair and urbane John Carter, at
Myron's right, had a pinch bottle of Haig and Haig; obviously a man of expensive tastes. The dark, curly-haired
Robert Dyke and the equally dark-haired, heavy-bosomed
Hedecai Schmidt, on Myron's left, were sharing a large
bottle of Israeli beer.

In between sneaking curious glances at him, the two students were carrying on an animated conversation in a subdued mutter. Otherwise the tent was very quiet. Outside of
introducing him as they had come straggling in to dinner,
Myron Goldsmith had volunteered no explanation of his
presence, nor for the moment was Toby about to volunteer
one. He was interested to see that Selwyn Grayson was
not of the company; he apparently was looking after himself. And his eyes dwelt curiously on the empty place by
which stood a bottle of plain mineral water; Ali-Muhammed, Bill's right-hand man by his position at the table, had
not arrived for the dinner call; in fact he did not seem to
be in camp at all. Again Toby wondered why.

John Carter looked toward him and cleared his throat
preparatory to breaking the social ice, when there suddenly came the explosive exchange of guttural Arabic outside the tent. The entrance flap parted to reveal the cook,
bearing a steaming platter, closely followed by a very
swarthy, well-muscled man clad in conventional digging
clothes. Seeing Toby sitting in the semidarkness at the end

of the table, he stopped dead, his dark eyes wide and startled. Then Myron slewed around in his chair and said something in Arabic with a very hostile undertone. The new arrival ignored him but advanced on Toby, a shaky smile set on the dark face. As the light caught him, Toby could see the beads of sweat starting on his brow.

The newcomer extended a hand that trembled slightly. "This is indeed an honor and a surprise, Professor Glendower. Bill has spoken so often of you. Ali-Muhammed at your service, sir. For a moment, seeing you sitting there, I thought our mutual good friend Bill Pierson had returned. Perhaps, though, you bring news of him?"

Toby took the extended hand and shook it gravely. "I had hoped that it was *you* who brought news," he rumbled. But the thought uppermost in his mind was why, on this chilly desert night, did this good friend of Bill's sweat as if he had just run a four-minute mile or had just seen a ghost?

CHAPTER 4

Penny always enjoyed her breakfast, as also, for that matter, her lunch, dinner and, occasionally, tea; she was therefore feeling a little put upon at having to share this pleasure with her new employer, who was using the occasion to submit Penny to a searching catechism.

It was a minor ordeal she had been spared the evening before, when Valerie had announced that she was exhausted from the trip and had not appeared for dinner. But now her energies had evidently been restored, and Penny was being hard put to retain the small store of sympathy she had worked up for the pale-faced woman sitting across the small, square table from her in the equally square, small, very Spartan dining room of the little hotel. She helped herself to more of the white, crumbly goat's-milk cheese and black olives to go with the excellent rye bread, and reflected gloomily that Toby was going to turn out to be right as usual, and that she would probably end up being very rude to the imperviously smug woman opposite to her.

"If you are an American by birth and upbringing, I really don't see why you've continued to live in England all these years, with all the *dreadful* times and taxes we have had to endure," Valerie was saying in her high, nasal whine. "Don't you like your own country?"

"I like it very much," Penny said with a slight edge to her voice, "but as I think I have already mentioned, my husband, Arthur Spring, *was* English, and I felt I owed it to his memory to bring up my son in the English way and in his father's country. Not that it worked out quite as I expected, but that was the general idea."

"Oh, in what way?"

"Well, Alexander, my son, turned out to be an unregenerate Yankee. A pure throwback, I'm afraid. Always

38

hated his English public school, and as soon as he could, he took off back to America, where he intends to stay and where he is now in the throes of becoming a doctor."

"How odd!" Valerie sniffed.

Penny, who saw nothing odd about it, bristled slightly and demanded, "Do you have any children?"

"Oh, *no!*" Valerie sounded faintly shocked at the very idea.

"Mmmph," said Penny. "Have some of this rose-petal jam, it's delicious. That toast you're eating looks as if it could use some help."

Valerie declined. She had opted for the English breakfast and was currently nibbling delicately on a dry-looking bit of baked bread. Refusing to be diverted from her train of thought, she went on, "And yet you still stay on in Oxford. Is that because you no longer have contacts in America or because of Toby?"

Penny, who long since had lost count of how many offers from American colleges she had turned down, did not rise to that one. "Oxford suits me very well," she said briefly, and gulped down the remainder of her tea. "I think I'd better get to work—that is, if you don't need me along for sightseeing or whatever."

"Oh, no, I thought I'd do some shopping," Valerie said, to Penny's surprise.

"Shopping!" The amazed ejaculation was out before Penny could stop it. Here was a woman supposedly worried to death about her husband's absence and she was going shopping!

"Yes," Valerie continued tranquilly. "I started a collection of *nargilehs*—water pipes, you know—when I was in North Africa, and when I was out here previously, I found a couple of *marvelous* little stores that have an amazing selection. What are you going to do?"

"Well, I am going to ask some questions around here and then strike out in ever-widening circles," said Penny, who only had the vaguest idea herself what she was planning. "I probably will be gone all day. Will you be all right?"

"Certainly. I'm expecting John Carter up from the dig today, to learn what's going on there so far. We'll probably have dinner together somewhere. John always knows the best places." And Penny noted with interest that Valerie seemed positively animated at the thought.

The hotel, as Penny had feared, did not yield much of interest to her. She tried to question the maids, only to find they spoke a minimal amount of English. Baffled by the language barrier, she had to resort to the manager, who was the only fluent linguist around but who was also somewhat wary about answering her questions. When she persisted, he grudgingly allowed her to examine the hotel register, but otherwise maintained that he knew nothing about anything or anybody.

The register was also unrevealing. Of the expedition party only Bill Pierson, Myron Goldsmith and Robert Dyke had stayed in the hotel. Hedecai Schmidt, Penny surmised, being an Israeli, had come direct from her home. The hotel probably was not grand enough for a Foreign Office type like Carter, and too grand for Bill's Arab sidekick, Ali-Muhammed. Wondering if there would be any point in finding out where they had stayed, she was idly turning the pages of the register when a familiar name caught her eye. "Hmm, that's interesting," she mused. "Selwyn Grayson stayed here. Bill's arch-rival. Toby certainly should be alerted to that. Let's see, he arrived here eight days ago and stayed here two nights. Puts him firmly on the spot just about the time Bill disappeared." Could there be a connection? She turned with an ingratiating smile to the manager, who was still hovering suspiciously. "I see a fellow countryman and old friend of mine was your guest here recently—a Mr. Grayson. Do you remember him and where he went? I would love to get in touch with him if he's around. Haven't seen him in years."

The manager unbent slightly. "Mr. Grayson? Oh, yes, I recall him. He did mention something . . . what was it now? I know it was something to do with his business. Locating something, I think, and he did mention a contact already here. But I'm afraid I cannot recall where he was going. He did have camping equipment with him, though, if that is of any help."

"I see." Penny was thoughtful. "That is very interesting. Thank you very much."

To be thorough, her next step was to visit the Depart-

ment of Antiquities, although she had not too much hope
of finding anything significant there, either. Here she
found everyone helpful and no language barrier, but unfortunately of little aid to her. All the business permits, labor
arrangements and general red tape surrounding an archaeological excavation had been handled by Myron Goldsmith. No one could recall even seeing Bill Pierson at any
stage of the business. As an afterthought, she asked, "Have
you, by any chance, had a visit from the director of antiquities in Algeria, Dr. Grayson? I believe he either is con-
templating or has already embarked on some work in
Israel." But this was met with blank stares. No one had
either seen or heard from Selwyn Grayson; whatever he
was doing in Israel, it was evidently on his own and totally
unofficial. Penny's interest began to mount.

With growing enthusiasm she decided to put off her
projected next stop at the British School of Archaeology
and instead went directly to the American School of Orien-
tal Research to follow up her lead on Selwyn Grayson. A
taxi deposited her before the impressive iron railings of
the American school on Saladin Road, standing stonily
solid, embowered in cypress trees in its handsome garden.
After some preliminary skirmishing with underlings, she finally got to see the assistant director, who was busy poring
over a vellum manuscript on his desk with a magnifying
glass.

He turned away from his task with reluctance and
greeted her with a vague smile. "Do sit down—er—Dr.
Spring, is it? My name is Garth Edwards. And what may
I do for you?"

He was a big, balding man with fair, much freckled
skin and ingenuous blue eyes, and it was evident that her
name meant nothing to him. Fair enough, Penny thought
wryly, for his name equally meant nothing to her. How
channelized we all are in our little worlds. "I rather hoped,
Dr. Edwards, you could give me some indication as to
where I might find Selwyn Grayson."

"Grayson, Grayson?" He wrinkled his freckled brow.
"Let me see. Something to do with Arabs. Yes, now I remember." He gave her a shy smile. "I'm afraid you're in
the wrong country. He works in Algeria."

"Yes, I know," Penny said patiently, "but at the moment he is here in Israel, possibly on archaeological business, and I'd like to locate him."

"*Is* he! Well, I'm afraid he hasn't been here," Garth Edwards said with a definite little shake of his head. "I'm sure someone would have told me about it if he had, what with the director being away, yes, I'm sure I would have been told . . ." he trailed off as his eyes riveted on the manuscript and stayed there.

Penny's heart sank. Obviously whatever Grayson was up to, he had not looked to his fellow countrymen for help. She got up. "Well, thank you for your time, Dr. Edwards. If he does come in, do you think you could let me know? I'm staying at the Sheikh Jarrah Hotel over on the Jericho Road."

"Of course," he murmured absently, "delighted," and by the time she had let herself out was once more completely oblivious to the present-day world.

Feeling increasingly frustrated, Penny hurried off to the British School of Archaeology, and here her luck appeared to run out completely. First of all she had a job finding anyone at all, and when she did and asked to see the director, she was told by a rather startled-looking secretary that everyone, including the director, was away digging on the current expedition site and would not be back for at least another month. Could she come back then?

No, Penny returned, she could not possibly wait that long. She needed information about the private British expedition at Wadi Mugharid, which she believed was also sponsored by the school, and wasn't there anybody at all about to whom she could talk?

The secretary, looking even more startled, said she'd see and disappeared, to return after a sizable interval looking relieved and with the message that the assistant librarian would be pleased to help in any way she could. She led Penny through the empty, echoing library to a small office beyond and announced with a small air of triumph, "Dr. Spring from Oxford University, Miss Cochran."

A blonde, fresh-faced woman, a little on the wrong side of forty, with a well-endowed figure running rapidly toward fat, rose to greet her. A pair of vivid blue eyes looked worriedly at Penny. "Margaret Cochran, Dr. Spring," she said. Her voice was warm, with a slight West Country burr to it. "You were asking about the Pierson expedition? You are an archaeologist from Oxford?" She sounded faintly puzzled.

"Well, no, I'm not." Penny took the chair indicated and smiled at her. "But I am a colleague of Sir Tobias Glendower, and I'm making some inquiries on his behalf because he is down at Wadi Mugharid."

"Sir Tobias at the dig!" Margaret Cochran was both impressed and astonished. "I knew, of course, that he and Bill Pierson were old friends, but I had no idea he was joining the expedition. Bill *will* be pleased."

Penny looked at her curiously. "He's not here for the dig, he's here to locate Bill."

"I'm afraid I don't understand," the blonde woman faltered.

"Bill Pierson's missing," Penny said gently. "He's been missing for almost a week. We're trying to find him."

All vestige of color left Margaret Cochran's face. She half-rose from her chair, clutching at the desk, and for a second Penny thought she was going to keel over in a dead faint. "Missing!" Margaret gasped. "Oh, no, that's not possible!" She slumped limply back into her seat.

"Are you all right? Put your head down for a minute," Penny said sharply. "Can I get you some water or something?"

She shook her head and made a little fending-off motion with her hands. "No, no, I'll be all right. It was a shock, that's all. So that's why . . ." She stopped abruptly and bit her lip.

Penny, looking at her with a keen eye, felt with a little surge of triumph that she had at last hit pay dirt. "You know Bill well?" she asked.

Margaret looked back at her dazedly. "We worked together on the Liverpool project for several years, right up until I came out here a year ago."

Aha! thought Penny in triumph. "Then you must know all about the people on the current expedition? Good! I need to know everything you can tell me about them."

The blonde, who apart from her hair color was about as opposite to Valerie Pierson as it was possible to be, pulled herself together. "I'm afraid I really do not understand what you are after, Dr. Spring. *Why* do you think Bill is missing, and what has Sir Tobias got to do with it?"

"Because Mrs. Pierson was so worried, she called him in to help. We all flew out yesterday."

Margaret Cochran's face closed in on herself, her full lips tightening to a thin line. "She's here? You are working with her?"

"Look," Penny said deliberately, "if it is any help, we don't care for Valerie Pierson any more than you appear to. Toby did not come out on her behalf but for *Bill*. You see, we know the *real* reason Bill was out here, and we also know that five days ago he took off in a Jeep and, according to the assistant director of the dig, has not been seen since. Knowing this, Toby is seriously worried. If you can help us, for God's sake do so, for if Bill has done what he set out to do, he may be in serious danger." She looked shrewdly at the ashen-faced woman across the desk. "If you worked with him on the Liverpool project, it is my guess that you know what he is after, too. This is no time to hold anything back—*help* us!"

She was unprepared for Margaret Cochran's next reaction. She shrank back, looking at her with horror-filled eyes. "Now I remember who you are," she gasped. "You're *that* Dr. Spring—the Pergama affair, the Cape Cod murders—my God! Do you think something has happened to Bill?" Her voice rose hysterically.

"I most sincerely hope not," Penny said sternly, trying to check the incipient hysteria, "but this is no time for cover-up or concealment. Believe me, anything you tell me, if it has no bearing on any of this, will never leave this room, but we simply have got to find out where he is and if he is all right. He may be somewhere out there in the Wilderness of Judea, injured and helpless, for all we know. If you know different, *tell* me!"

Tears welled up in the frightened eyes and spilled down the plump cheeks. "All right," Margaret sobbed, covering her face with her hands, "all right! I did know what Bill was after, and something must be wrong. I have been so worried . . ." She gulped and wiped away the tears with an improbably small handkerchief. "You see, Bill always contacted me when he came up from the dig. We usually had a meal together if he could manage it. Last time he was up, Valerie's boyfriend was with him so he could only phone . . ."

"Valerie's boyfriend!" Penny interjected in astonishment.

"Oh, yes! Valerie's old beau from East Africa, John Carter," Margaret said with venom. "You've no idea what Bill had to put up with. Though there are one or two things I could tell that bitch about her precious boyfriend . . ."

"Well, never mind that now," Penny cut in. "Go on about Bill."

"As I said, he could only phone. He was very excited. He said he was onto something big, even if it was not what he'd expected, but that it would mean we could do what we'd been planning—go off together, that is. He had enough on that bitch so she'd have to give him a divorce. He said he would be back in touch in a day or so, but then when I didn't hear and didn't hear . . ." The tears began to well again.

"And when was this?" Penny said hurriedly.

Margaret pressed the balled-up handkerchief to her lips. "A week ago," she sobbed.

"Did he say he had located Zadok's tomb?" Penny asked in excitement.

"No."

"Didn't he give you any indication what he had found?"

"No; just what I told you. But it must have been something important, something that was worth a lot of money. That's what we were waiting for—money. Bill hadn't any, nor I"—she shook her head hopelessly—"but he had to get away from that bitch before she ruined him entirely . . ."

There was a cold feeling about Penny's heart as she gazed with sympathy at the distraught woman. Bill Pierson had certainly sold her a bill of goods, but the big question was whether it was genuine. He had had one set of plans with his wife, another with this probably long-term girl friend, but could there be even a third set of plans with a younger, more attractive Miss X somewhere? "Then suppose we get down to cases," she said matter-of-factly, "and back to my original question. The people on the dig—were any of them in on it too?"

She got a violent shake of the head in reply. "No, I'm sure not."

"Not even this Ali-Muhammed?"

"No. Bill trusted him so far as looking after his interests on the dig was concerned, but they had been out of touch for a number of years, and he had heard rumors about Ali being in with the PLO here. He would never have trusted him with his secret after that."

"How about this Hedecai Schmidt? What do you know about her?"

"She is just an architecture student. She's from a kibbutz near Jericho originally. She volunteered her services at the school and Bill needed a draftsman for the site plans and drawings, so he took her on."

"You say she volunteered; is that usual?"

Margaret looked puzzled. "It is not *un*usual. Why, what are you getting at?"

"Nothing," Penny said hurriedly. "Just trying to get a clear picture, that's all. How about the rest of them?"

"The other student is an American, out on a grant from some foundation."

"You don't happen to know where he is from?" Penny inquired, seeing in her mind's eye the dark, curly-haired youth testifying in a sick voice about his finding the body in the bog.

"No, I'm afraid not. Bill said he was very pleasant but totally inexperienced, that's all."

"And Myron Goldsmith?"

"Well, Bill had to have him because of the London University grant. He said he was a good enough archaeologist, but a bit of a weak personality, and he had all sorts of headaches with him over Ali-Muhammed. Bill was *so* unlucky."

Penny was getting a little tired of this recurrent theme, so she pressed on. "And what about John Carter—couldn't he have known?"

Margaret looked at her in astonishment. "You've got to be joking! Bill could not stand him! He would never have told him in a million years. Carter invited himself on the dig and, since Valerie was footing some of the bill, Bill couldn't say no."

"Yes, but if Mrs. Pierson is as cozy with Carter as you say, *she* may have told him," Penny persisted.

"But she didn't know!" Margaret exploded.

Penny looked at her in silence for a moment. So Bill *had* been lying to both of them. "I'm afraid she did, you know," she said quietly. "She knew all about it, which is how we know, too. And if she told us, maybe she told Carter as well."

"I don't believe it," Margaret faltered. "I just don't believe it. There is no way she could have seen the scroll fragment. After all, *I* had it. I brought it out here with me. Bill was too careful to keep it himself."

"You've got it?" Penny said excitedly. "Then let's see it! It may give us a clue to where he is."

Margaret Cochran looked at her with dawning terror in her eyes. "I can't," she whispered. "You see, the last time I saw Bill, he took it with him. . . ."

CHAPTER 5

Toby was not in the best of moods. For one thing he was tired; whether it had been because of the somewhat greasy mutton stew, which had been the principal ingredient of dinner, or the unaccustomed lumpiness of the camp cot, he had not slept well. Usually, and totally unlike Penny, he was completely unaware of his physical surroundings, taking both luxurious and Spartan conditions equally in his absentminded stride, but last night had been different. He had slept only fitfully, starting into wakefulness under the impression that he had heard voices calling and movement of some kind, but when he had listened, there had been nothing but the chill whispering of the night wind.

To add to his irritability, he found he had left all his shaving tackle behind, and if there was one thing he detested above everything it was to start the day unshaven. He rubbed his hand over his itchy, stubbly face and half-heartedly rummaged through Bill's things, hoping to find his shaving gear. But he came up empty-handed and grumpier than ever.

For another thing he had already had a head-on collision with Myron Goldsmith. He had been amazed, and indeed horrified, to find that apart from a cursory search in the immediate environs of the camp and dig, no further effort had been made to locate Bill; and he had let this disapproving amazement show. This had irked the nervy Myron, who had snapped that he had conceived it his first duty to look after the dig and not to go cavorting off after a director who had neither the sense nor the manners to let anyone know where he was going. Matters were worsened when Toby had announced his firm intention of mounting a thorough search at once, and that he would be taking Tahir with him.

Myron angrily jumped on this idea. The dig was in bad enough shape; he could not consider letting the foreman go. If Toby wanted to go wandering in the wilderness, that was his business, but he certainly was not going to take Tahir with him.

Tahir, who had been an interested listener to all this, then broke in to say that he was not going to let Glendower-*bey* go into the desert by himself, and Myron Goldsmith could just go and chase himself (or less polite words to that effect). At this Myron had completely lost control and there had been a lot of shouting and arm waving before a compromise of sorts had been reached.

Toby had mooched gloomily over to the dig with his arm-waving companions and an accompanying cloud of Arab workmen. He had found it impeccably neat and totally uninteresting, but after a swift consultation with Tahir had made a few suggestions and had seen the workmen started on their day's activities before getting Myron's reluctant consent to Tahir's departure.

He had hoped to have John Carter along as well, but when he got back to camp it was to find that smooth gentleman spick and sparkling—which made Toby feel even worse and obviously with other plans for the day. He greeted Toby cheerfully. "Going to take a run to Jerusalem. Anything I can get or do for you there?"

Toby gave him a popeyed stare. "Are you taking the expedition Jeep?"

John Carter lit up a thin, elegant cheroot with an equally thin and elegant gold butane lighter, waved a hand vaguely in the direction of the Dead Sea and shook his head. "Oh, no. Brought my own bus along. Keep it down in the wadi below. Doesn't do to be stranded on this kind of thing, y'know." He came a little closer and dropped his voice to a confidential murmur. "Besides, I find a little of our Myron goes a long way, and being my own master . . ." He shrugged.

"I was going to ask you to come along, but if you have business in Jerusalem, of course that's out," Toby said casually.

John Carter shot him a shrewd glance. "Well, you know how it is with us Foreign Office types. Always on business even when we are supposed to be on leave, always something to keep a sharp eye on, eh what? Sun never really sets and all that . . ." He winked confidingly.

"I see. Yes, well, there is one thing you could do for me. I seem to have left all my shaving things behind. Could you contact Dr. Spring? She's staying at the Sheikh Jarrah Hotel with Mrs. Pierson. The things must be in the case I left with her."

"Right-oh, old chap." Toby winced. "Glad to. May drop in and see how poor old Val is holding up. Not that I think there is anything to worry about. She must be used to Bill's little flings by now."

Toby eyed him levelly. "Is that what you think has happened? Bill's just off on a bender because of the way things have been going here?"

Carter gave him a quick glance, then looked away. "No. Bill's not the bender type. More like some local bit of fluff has uttered a siren call." Sensing Toby's disapproval, he hurried on, "Not that it means anything, y'know. Bill always comes home to roost eventually."

"Have you anything concrete to base this on?" Toby said in a voice devoid of expression. "If you do know something, it would save us all a lot of time and trouble. *Do* you know where he went off to that day?"

"No. Sorry, haven't the faintest. Just know it's part of his pattern," Carter said hastily. "Well, I must be off. Probably won't be back till late, so don't wait up!" He strode jauntily off, the early sun striking gold from the fine, slightly-too-long hair.

Toby looked after him with gloomy disapproval. He had hoped from Valerie's description for something a lot better, but he was not too satisfied with John Carter. He could not quite put his finger on it, but there was something about him that did not jibe. For one thing, with all his impeccable grooming and natty dressing, Carter was no spring chicken. Toby put him at either the same age as himself or even a bit older. What had been striking good looks of the typically Anglo-Saxon, fair-haired, blue-eyed, square-chinned sort had not stood up well to the onslaughts of time. There were jowls around the fine line of the jaw, pouches under the blue eyes that were set just a little too close together. Though the fair skin was still fine, the features looked like a good wax cast that had melted slightly, blurring the outlines. And yet Carter was evidently not giving up the illusion of youth without a struggle; hence the rather jarring breeziness of his manner. He was like a leftover copy of a P. G. Wodehouse novel.

They had chatted casually over dinner the night before, and Carter had gone to some pains to impress on Toby his image as a successful diplomat. Outwardly he bore all the earmarks of it, but Toby, many of whose fellow Wyke-hamists had trodden the diplomatic path and were now, almost to a man, either ambassadors or ministers, knew a thing or two about the ways of the Foreign Office. From hearing Carter talk of his travels, he had deduced that he had never had what really could be considered a first-rate job, nor was he as far advanced in his career as his age indicated he should be. There was something wrong with him, but in which direction the flaw lay Toby had no idea.

A slight cough behind him brought him back to his present surroundings, and he turned to see the two students gazing anxiously at him. Robert Dyke, hopeful anticipation written on his young, undistinguished face, said, "We heard you were going to look for Dr. Pierson. Can we come along to help?" Hedecai Schmidt, standing stolidly beside him, gave an enthusiastic affirmative nod.

Toby hesitated. He did not wish to worsen the already bad relations with Goldsmith by still further denuding him of staff, and yet he had rather hoped to have a third pair of hands along. He had been stuck enough times in a Jeep in faraway places to know that with two people it was hopeless, with three it could be moved. He made a hasty compromise with himself, his basic misogynism taking over. "It is very kind of you to offer, Miss Schmidt," he rumbled placatingly, "but I feel you had better stay here. Dr. Goldsmith is very short-handed so he really will need you, and also we will be going into pretty rough country and I would not want to put you in any danger." She looked so crestfallen that he hurried on, "But it would be of enormous help to me if you would be good enough to take on Mr. Dyke's duties as well as your own. You see, if we get bogged down anywhere, a third man along would be invaluable." Hedecai, who was just about as stalwart as her male counterpart, looked faintly mutinous but nodded a reluctant consent.

To soothe her ruffled feelings still further, Toby hurried on, "And I believe you can give me some valuable information. I understand from Dr. Goldsmith that you were the last person to see Dr. Pierson. Could you tell me about that?"

"Yes, well, I had come back from the site a bit early to work a rough trench plan into better shape. I was in the drawing-and-finds tent." She waved a hand at one of the identical drab-green tents set at the end of a row. "Dr. Pierson came in and seemed surprised to see me, but then he asked me to go back to the site for the surveying theodolite he had left there. I thought it a bit odd, but of course I went, thinking he needed it right away. But then when I got back with it, he was gone."

"Did you hear or see him go?"

The young woman shook her head.

"Was there anyone else in camp at the time?"

"Everyone was out on the site except Ali-Muhammed; I've no idea where *he* was." Hedecai was faintly scornful. "As far as I know, I was the only one here."

Toby had questioned Ali-Muhammed about this at dinner the night before and had learned that he was checking the level in the ancient cistern that supplied the camp with its only fresh water and which was situated in the towering cliffs above them. He had stated that he had not seen Bill go, but that he thought he had heard the engine of a Jeep start up about four o'clock.

"What time was it when you got back to camp and found Dr. Pierson had gone?" Toby asked Hedecai.

"I can't be certain but I think it was around four o'clock."

At least that was one thing that checked, Toby thought. "And how did Dr. Pierson seem to you when you last saw him?" he said aloud.

Hedecai shrugged. "A bit uptight, but then he'd been like that for days."

"And how did you find him in general?" Toby asked, feeling horribly disloyal.

"He was very nice," Robert Dyke volunteered eagerly. "He took a lot of trouble with me, explaining things. This is my first dig, you know, and he was very patient."

Hedecai gave a sudden, unexpected giggle. "He was also a d.o.m."

Toby looked blank and Robert exclaimed in astonishment, "Really? You never told me that. But he's so old!"

"Oh, it's nothing serious, nothing I can't handle," Hedecai said with all the sangfroid of her nineteen years. "Just the occasional slap and tickle and a chase around the table. As a matter of fact," she confided to Toby, "I thought that's what I was in for when he appeared in the drawing tent. He had that sort of hot, glazed look that men get, you know? But it seems I was wrong."

Toby's heart sank a little further. A dirty old man—here was the recurring theme again: Bill as a woman chaser. It looked as if Penny might be right with her *cherchez la femme* idea, and he wondered fleetingly how she was doing in Jerusalem. He cleared his throat and turned his attention to Robert Dyke. "And you can add nothing to Miss Schmidt's memory of that day?"

"Not that day, no," Robert said slowly, "but there were a couple of other times I saw him taking off in the Jeep by himself. I don't know if that means anything."

"Which way did he go?"

"South. That's why I remembered it, because usually he'd head north either to Jericho or Jerusalem."

"South toward Engedi?"

Robert Dyke shook his head. "No, that's southeast from here. He seemed to be heading southwest, further into the desert, which puzzled me because there's nothing out there, is there?"

Toby's nerves tightened. "That might be very helpful. You are a very observant young man," he said with approval.

Robert grinned at him, his bright smile bringing sudden life to the plain, square face with its impossible snub nose. "That's how I managed to get here," he confided. "I got kind of interested in all this sort of stuff after I heard about what you and that lady anthropologist did on the Cape Cod murders. You see, I *found* that body in the bog, and when Mr. Dimola heard about it, he said that with my kind of observational powers I'd be a natural for archaeology. So here I am, sponsored by the Dimola Foundation. And I must say I wouldn't have missed this for the world. I sure hope I can help you find Dr. Pierson."

Toby almost groaned as another fear was realized and

Penny again proven right. "We can certainly use a pair of keen eyes out in the desert," he muttered. "But how did you happen on this particular dig? Through Dr. Grayson?"

Robert shook his head. "No. Never set eyes on him before he turned up here. Mr. Dimola has aided the Liverpool project with funds from time to time. He's very interested in the scrolls and he had heard of Dr. Pierson's dig."

Toby's eyes fixed reflectively on the orange tent, which was firmly zippered shut, with no sign of the owner or, for that matter, of the Land Rover. "Has either of you any idea where or when Dr. Grayson went off? He does not seem to be here."

They both looked blank and shook their heads. "Oh, well, no matter," Toby sighed. "We had better start loading my Jeep. We'll need plenty of water and enough food for a couple of meals. Can you take care of that?" He beckoned Tahir over. "There's an extra can of gas in my tent. Put that in and a shovel in case we have to dig ourselves out. Miss Schmidt, do you have any large-scale ordnance maps of the surrounding area you could let me have? All I have is a road map of Israel, and that won't be of much use where we are going."

"Yes, come over to the tent and I'll show you what we have." Hedecai was suddenly all business, and Toby shortly emerged armed with maps that covered most of the area between the camp and Engedi to the south and stretching in depth as far as Hebron in the west. The dismal thought again came to him that they might be embarking on a difficult and possibly dangerous wild-goose chase. He made his way over to the Jeep, where the two men, so strikingly different, were patiently awaiting him, but a figure emerged from one of the green tents and hurried purposefully toward him.

"Professor Glendower, a word with you!"

Ali-Muhammed in the bright morning sunlight looked a lot more prepossessing than he had the night before. He moved with smooth grace, his slim, wiry figure seeming to skim over the uneven ground, his finely chiseled features and dark olive skin standing out against the harsh yellow of the desert earth, bringing needed life to its aridity. He looked like a man very much at home in his environment and in command of it. Only when he was right up to him did Toby see that beneath the dark, almond-shaped eyes were darker circles, as if Ali also had passed a sleepless night. In fact, had Toby not known that he was a strict Muslim and therefore a teetotaler, he would have diagnosed a severe hangover. There was a sense of urgency about Ali as he leaned forward. "If you are going further into the wilderness to hunt for Dr. Pierson, I must warn you—it is very dangerous in there now."

"I'm taking all the usual things," Toby said mildly. "Plenty of water and gas, rations, snakebite kit . . . It is not the first time I've been in the desert, you know."

Ali gave an impatient snort. "I wasn't talking about that, though Allah knows the desert has enough dangers in that way, too. No, you'll need arms. Do you have a gun? You may need one. The Bedouin of this area do not take kindly to wanderers in their territory, and besides that, there is always the possibility of terrorist bands—not all of them Arab, I might add. You must go armed."

Toby shrugged. "Then we'll just have to take our chances. I have no gun. Unless you can provide one?"

"I do not have one, but Bill has." Ali lowered his voice. "He showed it to me and where he kept it hidden. I've no idea whether he smuggled it in or he got it here, but it's a big German Mauser. You should take that."

"Perhaps you're right," Toby said with reluctance. He was a peaceable man but was sufficiently in tune with the violence of the times to recognize well-meant advice when he heard it.

"Come, then, it is in your tent; I will show you." Ali glided away, Toby at his heels. Inside the greenish gloom of the tent, Ali went over to where two footlockers had been stacked to form a makeshift dressing table, removed the upper one and then fumbled in a small bag hanging from the tent pole, emerging with a key. He undid the padlock on the lower footlocker and removed the top tray. He dived confidently into the pile of clothes it contained and felt around. He shot a concerned glance at Toby and then removed all the clothes, feeling each article with mounting anxiety. "It *should* be here," he muttered, but when that search yielded nothing, he turned and went feverishly through the same process with the other footlocker, with no more success. Breathing hard, he squatted back on his heels and turned a startled face to Toby. "It is not here; it is gone. Bill must have taken it with him. I do not like this. I do not like this at all."

"Well, that settles that," Toby said in as even a tone as he could manage. But again he felt a sinking sense of foreboding; things were beginning to add up: no shaving tackle, no gun. Wherever Bill had gone, and for whatever reason, he had evidently gone well prepared.

CHAPTER 6

Toby had so much to think over that he did not want the added distraction of having to drive. Tahir confessed, rather wistfully, that he did not know how, but Robert Dyke immediately and cheerfully volunteered although he had never handled a four-wheel-drive before. Silently blessing the universal mechanical preparedness of American youth, Toby climbed into the back seat of the Jeep with all the other baggage, and they jolted unsteadily away from the camp while young Robert got the hang of the gears.

The path they were following to the southwest was trackless, but that, Toby realized, was of no significance. He had already observed that the night wind off the Dead Sea, which appeared to be a constant of the area, drove the coarse-grained desert earth like a fine rain over every surface, and covered up each night all the marks that man had made upon its yielding surface during the still, daylight hours.

Tahir in the front seat began to hum to himself like a gigantic humblebee, eventually breaking out into the wailing, harsh cadences of an Arab love song. Toby looked at the back of the big man, his huge calloused hands braced against the metal dashboard to steady himself from the bone-jarring jolting, and realized that he was completely happy; a free man going back to the freedom he knew best—the desert.

He looked over his shoulder at the harsh, unrelenting landscape and wished he could feel the same. As far as the eye could see, the Wilderness of Judea stretched in tormented upheaval of craggy cliff and purple-shadowed gully, glinting a harsh gold in the high morning sun; not a tree, not a blade of grass was visible. Far off on its hilltop the stark outlines of the fortress of Masada could be seen, peopled by its brave ghosts but as empty now of the living as all the rest of that burning, arid land. To the southeast

Toby could make out the small patch of green that marked the oasis of Engedi and the slim ribbon of a road that wound along the shore by the metallic blue of the Dead Sea toward its promise of fruitfulness. And across that inland sea, so starkly devoid of life, the Mountains of Moab showed mistily purple blue under the cloudless sky.

Unlike most Englishmen Toby had no empathy for the desert. Although he would have been the last to admit it, his Celtic blood demanded green hills and greener valleys. He had come to terms in his life with the harsher realities of the Mediterranean landscapes, the starkness of white limestone and of dusty green olive groves, but with the desert—never. It frightened him, intimidated him, reduced him; yet he knew he must come to terms with it, too, must force it to yield up its secrets if he were ever to find his friend.

The Jeep had been climbing a slight rise and now came to a jerky halt as Robert Dyke said uncertainly, "Which way should we head, do you think, sir?"

Toby came out of his reverie to see that the wadi gully they had been following had split here into three narrower ones, all climbing quite steeply toward a flatter massif of cliff ahead. A sense of helplessness seized him as his imagination split the three into three more and so on and on ad infinitum. They could wander in this maze forever; they could pass within a few yards of Bill lying helpless or dead and never be any the wiser. It was hopeless. . . . He took a stern hold on himself and cleared his throat. "Let's take a break here while I look at the map. I couldn't see with the Jeep in motion." He passed the water canteen to Robert, and Tahir, with something akin to a snort, jumped out of the Jeep and strode off behind a nearby rock.

He spread the map out on his knees and tried to focus his thoughts. He must go on the assumption, lacking a better one, that Bill was after the treasure and therefore Zadok's tomb. The tomb, according to Josephus, had been located in a garden, ergo *if* it were located in the wilderness at all, that meant an oasis. There were only two known in the area—Ain Feshta, which lay behind them and in the wrong direction, and Engedi ahead but to the southeast. But Bill had headed southwest. Perhaps then a former oasis now dry. And the most likely place for that?

Toby looked hard at the map and started to draw some lines on it. The water that supplied the springs of Engedi down the large wadi that lay due west of it must come from somewhere on the massif directly in front of them, or possibly the one on the more southerly side of the wadi. First things first; they were here, so this massif was number one on the agenda. A garden would most probably be where a spring rose *from* the massif at the source. He thought of pictures he had seen of miniature waterfalls pouring down the rock faces of Masada in the rainy season to fill its ancient cisterns, but rejected that possibility as being too precarious a basis for the establishment of a permanent garden; no, they must look for the source.

He drew some lines from their present position and noted where they intersected with the hypothetical lines of water supply he had drawn from Engedi. "We'll try the most westerly branch first," he said firmly, "and if that does not work out, we'll come back here and start again. Tahir!"

The Kurd reappeared from behind the rock, gave Toby a savage grin and rebraced himself as the Jeep started up in low gear. For some time they jolted onward and upward in silence, the walls of the wadi towering over them and cutting off the view. To the left the cliff was unbroken, but to the right many subsidiary gullies came in at an angle. The further in they went, the wider the main wadi opened out. Toby felt this might be a good sign but said nothing, for he was not about to raise any false hopes.

It was now uncomfortably hot. The sun almost directly overhead banished shadows, so that Toby's eyes ached with the glare from the tarnished gold cliffs, and he sweated from the heat bouncing off the shale walls. His glasses kept misting up, making his own observation useless, and he was just about to suggest stopping and having some lunch until the sun had passed its zenith when Robert Dyke braked sharply and began to back up. "What's up?" Toby demanded irritably.

"I thought I saw something back there in that last gully." The young man was excited. "Something that did not look like a rock. I think we ought to take a closer look."

Toby took off his glasses, wiped the sweat from his eyes and carefully polished the round lenses before putting them on again. He peered ahead. The narrow gully they had pulled into, the Jeep shrieking its protest, was strewn with large rocks and some bushes and coarse tufts of grass, indicating at least some water. It did not look very promising, but a squarish shape at the side of the gully and further in which did not conform to the jagged rocks around it caught his eye. "Right," he said sharply. "Stop the Jeep. No sense in risking an axle with all these rocks about. We'll walk in."

He climbed stiffly out and led the way, picking his route through the tumbled rocks and underbrush. As he neared the object, his steps quickened and his heart sank. It was a Jeep, or at least what was left of one. They came up to it and gazed in silence. It had been systematically stripped; wheels, tires, mirrors, the windshield, even the seats had been removed. It stood forlorn, a metal carcass picked clean by human vultures. Toby glanced at the other two men. "Well? Is it Dr. Pierson's?" he demanded.

Tahir shrugged. "It could be, *effendi,* but how could one tell?"

Robert swung himself up into it and began scrabbling energetically in the stripped interior, tossing out dead branches and handfuls of grass that partially disguised it. "Must have been here some time," he commented. "The dust over everything is thick." Finding nothing to interest him, he jumped down again and opened up the hood to peer at the cold engine. "Looks okay to me. I wonder . . ." He got out a folding measuring stick from his pocket and dipped it into the gas tank. "Not out of gas, though there's not much left in it. Could have been siphoned off, I suppose." He went through the same performance with the radiator. "Plenty of water in that." He frowned. "No keys, but do you want me to jump the ignition, sir, to see if it will start?"

"To what purpose?" Toby asked gloomily. "The one thing we need to know about it—whether it is Bill Pierson's—apparently cannot be answered. Get the engine number. The only thing we can do is check on it when we get back to camp or to Jerusalem, where, presumably, Dr. Pierson hired or borrowed the expedition vehicles."

"Well, if we found out whether it worked, we would at least know if he had abandoned it and had to go off on foot. Or, if it *does* work, it would indicate that perhaps he was waylaid by whoever did the stripping," Robert continued with admirable logic. He looked up at the towering cliffs above the wadi. "There are some caves up there. Want me to go up and have a look around in case they cached the stuff from the Jeep in one of them? Then maybe we could tell definitely."

"I had noticed the caves," Toby put in dryly. "And later, maybe, for both projects, but for now I think it would be a good idea if we went back, had some lunch and rested a bit until this heat cools a little. Those cliffs will need some scaling by the looks of them. No sense in getting heat prostration in the process."

He turned to lead the way back and halted in sudden shock. They were no longer alone in the wilderness. Standing between them and their own Jeep were four silent figures, their long, flowing black robes and white burnooses adding a biblical touch to the barren landscape. But there was nothing remotely biblical about the rifles two of them were holding or the knives that glinted in the belts of the other two.

Tahir muttered a soft ejaculation under his breath and then said in Turkish to Toby, "I don't like the looks of this. You and the young one stay here. I'll do the talking; don't you say a word."

Toby answered in the same tongue. "No, we'll stay together; otherwise they might jump you. One thing for sure—we'll have to talk our way out or not get out at all." In English he said to the wide-eyed Robert, "Looks as if we've got some native company. Stick close to us, and if you've got anything valuable on you, drop it *very* surreptitiously here. You can get it later." I hope, he added to himself.

Tahir eased his own large knife into plain sight, took the lead and swaggered confidently off toward the watchful group, Toby and Robert close behind. As they came up to the silent Arabs, he raised a hand in greeting and boomed out a salutation. *"Salaam aleikum."*

"Aleikum salaam," came the communal mutter as four pairs of dark, suspicious eyes surveyed them from top to toe. Three of the Bedouin were heavily bearded and of indeterminate age. The fourth member, taller than the others, was young and beardless, with a proud, hawklike

face; he appeared, despite his youth, to be their leader.
He rapped out a guttural query at Tahir, who drew himself
up to his full height so that he towered over the group, but
he kept a pleasant smile on his lips as he returned a pacific
answer.

The tempo of the exchange picked up, and Toby was
only able to make out a word here and there—*Jew,
brother, English, Hussein, cave, Lawrence*—but nothing
connected, and he had no way of telling how the conversation was turning. The exchange grew more heated and
arms began to wave; the three other Arabs began to move
restlessly and Toby kept a close, intimidating blue eye on
them as their dark glances skittered over him and Robert
standing stolidly by his side, his square chin thrust de-
fiantly out.

Irrelevant thoughts kept popping into Toby's head. He
was thankful now that Penny had firmly confiscated his
signet ring and expensive gold watch to keep for him, and
had made him wear his old dig watch with its built-in
compass. If these Arabs were up to no good, at least their
booty would be slim so far as he was concerned. He tried
to remember where he had put his will and failed. He
wondered who would finish the report on his last excavation at Troezen. And most of all he wondered how, if
things got rough, he could distract them long enough to
let young Robert get away.

Suddenly Tahir held up his arms in a dramatic gesture
for silence and turned to him, still with the set smile on
his lips but warning in his eyes. Toby could see beads of
sweat on the dark brow under the loose blue turban. "We
are in the territory of these men, *effendi*," Tahir said slowly
and carefully in English, "and they ask what we do here.
I have told them that you and your son, beside you, seek
your brother, who has been missing in this desert some
several days past, and that I guide you. I have told them
they must know you are an Englishman and so a great
friend of their people, like the great Lawrence-*pasha*, and
that you are a friend of King Hussein since many years
and come to seek your brother from his palace. So great
a friend that, if you should not return, he would send
many men to seek you, even though this be the country
of the Jews. These Bedouin here understand what it is to

be worried about a brother, for they have many in Jordan beyond the border and worry about them, too. I have asked if they know anything of your brother, or of the Jeep back there, but they say they know nothing. I have asked them about the caves around us, but they say they are empty and of no interest to anyone. They also say this is a dangerous place, particularly when the darkness comes, and since they do not wish you to become lost like your brother, they advise us to be gone by nightfall. They also say they are hungry and could we give them food."

Toby cleared his dry throat, took up his cue and put on his most pontifical rumble. From Tahir's manner of speaking, he had gathered that the big Kurd suspected that at least one of them understood English and was being careful not to make them any more suspicious or hostile than they already were. "I am thankful for the help of these respected men," he returned, "and will indeed tell my friend, the king, of their kindness. Be so good as to give them what food we have in our Jeep, saving only that which we shall need ourselves for our noonday meal, as a small return for their concern for us. We will search for my brother while the light lasts and then will return whence we came."

Tahir nodded, a glint of laughter in his dark eyes, and strode over to the Jeep, closely followed by two of the Arabs. They returned with their arms full of provisions, and one of them, who had been covetously eyeing the binoculars slung around Toby's neck, said something in a low voice to their young leader. He replied with a curt negative and then swung around to Tahir. "You go by nightfall," he stated in harsh, heavily accented English, and with a swirl of black robes the group strode out of the wadi, turning in a northerly direction.

Toby felt weak with relief. Leaning against the Jeep, he carefully filled and lit his pipe. Tahir came and leaned on it beside him. "That was close," he murmured. "I think we should get out of here right now before they change their minds."

Toby exhaled a fragrant blue cloud and shook his head. "I don't think so. If we rush away from here, they'll think we were lying and will waylay us anyway. If we do as I said we would, they may leave us alone. I expect they will be watching for us on the road. They are between us and the camp." He beckoned to Robert, who was looking bewildered. "We'd better eat whatever they have left us now," he growled. "Then if you are in the mood for some mountain climbing, you can start going through the caves up there. It will save us some time. Tahir and I will join you as soon as we have got our breath back."

They shared out what was left of the food and ate and drank in silence, uneasily conscious that eyes might be upon them. As soon as Robert was finished, Toby unslung his binoculars and handed them to him. "Off you go. Got your flashlight? Give us a shout if you find anything. And careful as you go; the last thing we need now is for you to break a leg. We'll be up presently."

The young man bounded off like a greyhound out of its starting gate. Tahir leaned back against the Jeep and chuckled. "You even begin to sound like a father, *effendi.*"

Toby looked pained. Then, becoming serious, Tahir went on, scuffing at the dusty earth with his big, soft leather boots, "I suppose you noticed the sandals on those men?"

Toby nodded. "Yes, made of rubber from tires and brand-new by the look of them. You think they stripped the Jeep?"

"Most probably. This is what they think of as their land, and anything in it is theirs by right."

"Do you think they may have done something to Dr. Pierson, *if* that is his Jeep?"

Tahir squinted up at the sun, now past its meridian and beginning its steady, shadow-casting march down the sky. "I would not say so, no. To rob a man is one thing, to kill him another—particularly if he offers no resistance, no threat."

Toby thought of the missing gun and kept an uneasy silence.

"One of the men had a European watch," Tahir observed, "but I could not say if it was Pierson-*bey*'s. But I do not think these are the killing kind, or we might be now all in the dust."

"But to silence those whom they rob?"

"No. Why should they? They do not fear the Israeli

authorities, for they know they cannot police this wilderness, and to try to capture a Bedouin is like trying to seize the wind. But the Bedouin do not seek trouble with them, either. If they kill, it would have to be for a reason, and a good one at that."

Searching for and perhaps finding treasure might be reason enough, Toby thought despondently, and his unease increased. "I think we'd better get moving," he said gruffly, "and give young Robert a hand. A good lad, that; didn't show any signs of panic."

"Yes, a fine son," Tahir teased cheerfully, and began to mount the cliff face with an agility that left Toby gasping. He toiled up behind him until they reached a narrow ledge of harder rock that formed a natural pathway along the ins and outs of the whole cliff face, and along which could be seen the dark clefts of caves.

Toby paused to get his breath back and wheezed, "We'd better give him a shout to see how far he has got. No sense in going over the same ground."

But scarcely were the words out of his mouth before a faint and frantic shouting began, and as they started toward it, they saw Robert Dyke appear around a spur of the cliff and come haring along the narrow path at breakneck speed. His face was greenish white and streaming with sweat, his eyes wide and panic-stricken. "Oh, God!" he choked out as he stumbled toward them, "I've done it again! I've found a body. It's in a cave back there." And, leaning weakly against a rock, for the second time in his young life, he saluted the occasion by vomiting his recent lunch back into the wadi below.

CHAPTER 7

"*Y'Allah,* he has killed himself." Tahir's deep voice sank even lower in the scale as their flashlights played an eerie tattoo on the mortal remains that lay crumpled on the floor of the dark cave, a gun clutched in one of the contorted dead hands. He went to push aside the big boulder partially blocking the narrow cleft that was its entrance preparatory to going in, but Toby grasped at his arm.

"No, not yet." Even in his state of shock, Toby's mind was still registering, observing details that relayed an even grimmer message. "We must be very careful. Look at his wrists!" He pinpointed the flashlight on them and on the great bands of black, congealed blood that ran around each one. "He's been bound with ropes that cut into the flesh. It could be murder. We must watch where we step; there may be footprints." The flashlight moved over the gritty floor, but here too the desert wind had done its work and there were just traces in the surface, but no discernible track. Bitter gall welled up into Toby's throat and he said thickly, "Too late to matter. We may as well go in."

With a convulsive heave the big Kurd moved the blocking boulder. They squeezed through the narrow cleft into the cave, which ran long and narrow within the cliff face, with several darker fissures leading off into deeper blackness from the back wall. They stood in silence for a moment on either side of the body, their tall figures throwing grotesque shadows on the cave walls. In Toby's heart was bitter anger as he gazed down on the body of his old friend.

Bill Pierson lay with his head cushioned on his right arm, half-turned toward the entrance. In his right hand was the gun. The dead eyes were half-open, the eyeballs glinting whitely in a ghastly semblance of life. Before Toby could stop him, Tahir had rolled the limp body over on its back and with a swift movement closed the dead eyelids.

Toby sucked in his breath sharply. "Murdered!" he said, and Tahir recoiled. A round hole circled by blackened blood showed in the tanned column of the throat. There was another just above the heart; but that was not the worst of it. The khaki shirt had been unbuttoned, and with the turning of the body had fallen open to reveal the chest and stomach, which were covered by the scars of burns. "Tortured and murdered!"

With an exclamation of disgust Tahir squatted by the body and gently pulled open the trousers, which were unbuttoned. There was a grumble of anger in his throat as he revealed further horror. The entire genital area had been scorched and burned, the burnt hair still giving off its distinctive acrid odor. "What kind of devil could do this?" the big Kurd grunted.

Toby turned his head away. "You'd better get back to the Jeep," he said unsteadily. "Have young Robert take you to the police post at Engedi. Leave him there, but bring them back with you." After the shaken boy had shown them the cave, they had sent him back, ostensibly to guard the Jeep but in actuality to give him time to pull himself together after his gruesome discovery.

The big man got to his feet. "But what about you, *effendi?*"

"I'll stay here and guard the body."

"It may not be safe. Let me stay."

"No. For one thing, you can explain things better in Hebrew than I. There may not be an English speaker at the post. For another, you can find the way quicker. I'll be all right."

Tahir unsheathed his big knife and held it out to him. "Take this; you may need it."

Toby looked at it for a second, its long blade gleaming wickedly in the dim light. "You think the Bedouin did this?"

"Never!" Tahir roared. "To beat a man, to cut, perhaps. But this filthiness? Never! No man who walks in the fear of Allah would do such."

Not even if the stakes were high enough? Toby thought, but rejected it, for how could the Arabs have known what had been in Bill's mind. "I'm inclined to agree with you," he said slowly. "But you keep the knife." He gave a grimace of distaste. "After all, there is the gun I can use. Go quickly now."

Tahir hovered uncertainly for a moment, a wild light in his large dark eyes, then hurled himself out of the cave. Toby could hear the thudding of his boots like a soft drumbeat along the outer wall as he ran back down the narrow path. He gave a shuddering sigh and turned his unwilling gaze back to the body. The missing gun was explained, and so, for that matter, was the absence of shaving tackle; sometime since their last meeting Bill had grown a full beard, which partly masked the final agony on his face. It was a possibility that had not even occurred to Toby.

Overcoming his distaste, he knelt beside the body. His anger was cold now, and he was determined that whoever had done this to Bill should be made to pay. With a sense of savage satisfaction, he remembered that the Israelis still had the death penalty; not that that would make up for what Bill had endured, but at least it was something.

Since the Pergama affair Toby had done a lot of quiet reading on forensic medicine, though he had never thought to use such arcane knowledge on the body of a friend. He tested the arm gently; all signs of rigor mortis had disappeared, but, save for a well-established lividity on the side on which the body had been lying, there was not much evidence for the start of decomposition. Part of this, he supposed, might be due to the extreme aridity of the atmosphere of the cave, but as a rough estimate he did not think Bill had been dead for more than forty-eight hours.

Two days ago, when he was on his way to Israel on his vain mission of mercy, someone had stood over Bill's tortured, helpless body and pumped two bullets into it. Why? Because they had extorted from him what they wanted, or because they did not dare wait any longer, knowing a search for him was to be made?

And for the four days before that, supposing his torturer had made his move on that first day? His mind revolted at the idea of what Bill had endured in that time. Steeling himself, he bent forward to examine the mutilations more closely. The corners of the mouth under the bushy beard were rubbed raw from savage gagging, the lips swollen, blackened and bitten almost through from the agonies endured; the lacerated wrists bore further mute testimony to the body's writhings under this torment of fire.

His interest quickened as he examined the burns. There was a shape to them he had not noticed before, a deeper indentation surrounded by blackened skin; the tip of something round—a cigarette, a cigar, or a round metal object—the autopsy should be able to tell which. But no cigarette could have done that to the genitals. That horror came from a larger flame; a brand, perhaps.

But there was no sign of such in the dirt of the cave floor, and he was aware of some other odor besides that of the burnt hair and stale urine; one which he could not identify for the moment but which teased familiarly at his mind. Again he would have to direct the attention of the police to this anomaly.

Feeling suddenly nauseated, he got up in a hurry and made for the cave entrance, where he propped himself against the boulder to get a grip on himself. He reached for the automatic comfort of his pipe, which he had some difficulty in lighting. He realized his bush jacket was wringing wet with his own sweat, so his matches were damp, and it did not help matters that his hands were shaking. With an effort of will he steadied himself and looked out over the wadi. Why had the murderer made that absurd and clumsy attempt to make it look like suicide?

The answer came like a lightning flash. Obviously it was because the murderer did not anticipate that the body would be found for a very long time; not until it was a skeleton. On a skeleton what would be left? Nothing but the gun in the hand and two bullets; no telltale marks of the bonds or of the torture.

His eyes strayed to the deserted Jeep which was about a hundred yards down the wadi toward the entrance by which they had come in. Why, then, if the killer had banked on the body *not* being discovered, had he not removed that piece of telltale evidence, without which—and without young Robert's eagle eye—their attention would never have been drawn to this particular place?

Without this mute signpost the body probably would never have been found.

His eyes narrowed as a possible solution occurred to him. If the Bedouin had done this thing—and he was inclined to agree with Tahir and rule them out—they would certainly have moved the Jeep elsewhere before stripping it. But the murderer had not done so—why? Because for some reason he *couldn't*.

Toby sighed and backtracked. Supposing the murderer was someone on the expedition or connected with it; where did that lead? Bill had left the camp alone in the Jeep, so the murderer must have had a vehicle, too; must have followed him somehow. Then Bill was attacked, left bound and helpless in the cave. But the murderer would then have had two vehicles to deal with, his own and Bill's. Presumably he went off to deal with his own, intending to return later to take care of Bill's, and perhaps also because he did not wish to arouse suspicion by an overlong absence. He returned to find that an unkind fate had intervened: in the meantime the Bedouin had found the Jeep and stripped it so that it could not be moved. So he had disguised it as well as he could with branches and dirt and hoped it would not be discovered until time had done its deadly work on the body. Vain hope!

Then who? Toby got out his black notebook and started to marshal his thoughts. Of the expedition staff he ruled out the two students automatically, Robert for obvious reasons and Hedecai because she was female. His eyes dwelt on the cave entrance and the boulder against which he was propped; a deeper groove in the earth of the ledge indicated clearly how the boulder had been moved into place to effectively block that narrow entrance and that Tahir had moved it back almost to its original position. It had been no easy task for the big man and so was beyond the strength of any normal woman; so Hedecai was out. He was about to add Tahir to the impossibles list when his pen wavered. His theory of the Jeep had been based on the supposition of another driver and another car, but there was a flaw in it. What if the Jeep had not been moved because the murderer couldn't drive? Tahir was a nondriver.

Toby tried to estimate how far they had come from the

camp; not more than seventeen miles at most, for the going had been very slow, and possibly it was a lot less across country. In his mind's eye he could see the graceful speed of the big Kurd as his long legs devoured distance; to a mountain man like him, fifteen miles would be as nothing. No, although his mind revolted against the thought, he could not add Tahir to the impossibles list as yet.

With a sigh he went on writing. Myron Goldsmith. Physically on the small side but wiry; would probably have enough strength. Opportunity? Had to be checked, but there was at least one occasion on which he was away from camp by himself—the time he had phoned Mrs. Pierson from Jerusalem. How long had he been gone that day? Check for other absences. Motive? Resentful of Bill as leader, Toby wrote, got wind of treasure hunt? Heavy drinker; problems from this? But he found it hard to imagine Myron doing what had been done to Bill.

Selwyn Grayson. Toby paused. Now here was a more realistic possibility. Bill's hated rival. Turned up without explanation three days ago and was hanging around. For what? The treasure? Selwyn had always had a reputation for ruthlessness and had been involved with some shady characters in his time. He also had his own equipment and transport, and could come and go as he pleased. Double-check on him.

Ali-Muhammed. Supposedly Bill's friend, but was he? Toby remembered his very strange reaction to his presence in Bill's seat the night before. And Myron had mentioned his frequent absences. But then the business of the gun this morning made no sense; why, if Ali-Muhammed were involved, would he draw attention to it at all? Yet of all the people there he was the one most likely to have got wind of what Bill was really up to, being closest to him, and he had ready access to expedition vehicles.

John Carter. Possibly a loser in his career and a loser with evidently expensive tastes. Check financial position. Old friend of both the Piersons, so could also have got some wind of what was going on from one or both of them. Had his own transport and again could come and go as he pleased.

Toby looked grimly at the list; all of them possibilities, but there was also always the possibility of an outside and unknown factor. In his small, neat handwriting he made a final entry—Mr. X—and shut the notebook with a snap. He stowed it away and, crossing his arms, puffed vigorously on his pipe, looking out across the wadi where the shadows were now deepening and lengthening. The Jeep was now in dark shade and invisible. He glanced at his watch and realized that it would still be some time before he could realistically expect Tahir to get back with the police; he might as well put the time to some use. He would have another look at the cave and see if he could find any clues to the murderer's presence.

This time he avoided the body and directed his flashlight on the outer perimeters of the cave. At the edge of one of the fissures, something caught his eye. He knelt down to examine it closer; lying there in a final curl of defiance and clearly identifiable was a scorpion's stinger, the rest of the body in tiny fragments around it where they had been ground savagely into the dust by a booted heel. More important, the imprint of the heel had been ground so deep that the filtering dust had not as yet totally obscured it. The faint pattern could still be made out. It was a ribbed heel, possibly of crepe rubber, Toby thought. He trained the light on Bill's boots, which showed plain leather soles; so not his, but in all probability his tormentor's. He wished fervently that he had his camera along. He did the next best thing and sketched the imprint. "Let's hope the police bring some equipment," he grumbled to himself as he continued his painstaking, inch-by-inch search. The second and larger fissure offered grim if intangible evidence; it had been the torture chamber.

Two sizable rocks were positioned one on each side of the narrow cleft. A third lay in the middle of it about nine feet in from the other two, and between them the earth was much disturbed. Bill had evidently been spread-eagled here, his boots pinned between the rocks and the cave wall, his bound wrists placed around the rock in the middle. There were traces of leather on both the rock and the wall where the boots had scraped as the tortured man had writhed in his agonies, and by the third rock were dark stains in the earth where his bound wrists had bled. Toby started to feel sick again but fought it down. If a cigarette or cigar had been used to inflict those burns, there should be ash from them, and ash could be identified. He leaned in, trying not to disturb the surface, and peered closely at the earth. In one or two places he thought he could detect a grayer, finer dust. He groped in his pockets for anything that would hold a sample, located an old envelope and carefully scraped some of the finer dust into it, being equally careful to leave plenty for the Israeli police. He certainly was the last one to wish to destroy any possible evidence. With a thankful grunt he switched his flashlight away from the cleft, which to his overwrought nerves still housed a brooding sense of horrific terror.

The third fissure also produced its yield, which served to steady him again, for this evidence was of a kind he could understand. Scattered across the floor were broken shards of a large, coarse pot, which Toby immediately recognized as a "scroll" pot, one of the large earthenware vessels in which so many of the scrolls had been found. He picked up one of the bits and examined the edges carefully. It was hard to say definitely, but he could almost swear that the breakings were comparatively recent. Excitement seized him; what if Bill had stumbled onto something else during his quest? What if he had found a new scroll? It would completely alter the whole picture. He pocketed the shard he held for future dating and, getting out his penknife, began to scrape energetically around the other bits of pot; just a scrap of vellum or metal would give him some idea if he was on a brand-new trail. His knife hit something that yielded, and he very gingerly eased out a small object from under the edge of one of the potsherds. He held it close to the light, which was now turning yellow and beginning to dim. It was a fragment no more than an inch square but unmistakably of vellum. To add to his excitement, it had on it traces of black ink.

In his haste to examine it by better light, he almost stumbled backward over the body. This shocked him into a more rational state and grimmer reality. His friend was lying murdered at his feet, and here he was getting all steamed up about a tiny scrap of rubbish! A fine friend he was!

For the first time a tremendous wave of sadness engulfed him as he gazed down at the huddled figure; so many memories, so many dreams they had shared. Bill's solemn young face was in his mind, eagerly assuring him, "I'm going to make it to the top, Toby, right to the top I'm going. We'll be the ones they remember from *this* century, just you wait and see!" Poor, vain, hopeful Bill—for what now would he be remembered?

His eyes suddenly narrowed as an anomaly struck him. Bill's clothes had been thoroughly searched by his abductor. One of the pockets of his safari-style shirt was actually ripped down and his pants pockets turned inside out; yet his toupee, the very first place Toby would have looked for something hidden, was still securely in place on his head.

Bill's hairpiece had always been a source of secret amusement to Toby, whose own fine thatch of silver hair was his one claim to beauty. Bill's hair had started to retreat early, and by the time he was in North Africa, he had been partially bald, a fact which had fretted him enormously. Apparently it had finally irked Valerie, too, because Toby had been surprised and somewhat shocked when he had visited them in East Africa to find Bill with a full and splendid head of hair again. Bill had bashfully admitted to the toupee, putting the weight of its existence to Valerie's credit but obviously delighted by the whole thing. And Toby had never seen him without it since that time.

"I wonder," he murmured softly, and knelt beside the body. He ran his hands through the dark hair, feeling for the telltale outlines of the hairpiece, and gave it a gentle tug. It yielded slightly but stayed in place. Grimacing with distaste, Toby gave it a stronger tug and it came away, leaving the pallid gleam of bare flesh beneath. It smelled sourly of soaked sweat, but when Toby held it up to the by now dim glow of the flashlight, his heart skipped a beat. A pocket running the length of the hairpiece had been sewn onto it, and in that pocket his questing fingers encountered something that yielded to his touch. A few long strides took him to the mouth of the cave and the light of late afternoon. His hands were trembling so he could scarcely disengage the stuck and matted contents from their hiding place. By the time he unrolled and carefully smoothed all the creases inch by painful inch, he was dripping with sweat himself, but by spreading it out on the boulder's surface, he had managed it without a single break or tear. He was holding a piece of vellum six inches long by about five wide, torn raggedly all around but with the lower left-hand edge particularly jagged. It was covered with writing. His eyes tried to focus on the jet black characters as his mind whirled in excited chaos.

His thoughts were so fixed on Zadok's treasure that he struggled to make sense out of the script in terms of words he might recognize in Hebrew such as *north, south,* or *Zadok.* It took him some time to realize that what he was gazing at so intensely was, in fact, arranged in two columns and in two different hands, and that one of the hands was written in a language that he understood. It was a list in Latin.

Two names leaped out at him as his mind finally seized on this, and his eyes widened in shock. One name read JUDAS, PATER IGNOTUS, NOMINATUS ISCARIOT; the other, JESUS, FILIUS JOSEPHUS, NAZARETH.

CHAPTER 8

There had been no time to digest his amazing find. From the wadi below, deep now in shadow, came the tramping of booted feet and the murmur of voices. Toby realized belatedly that he had done an unforgivable thing in interfering with the body. But he was not about to let this precious find out of his possession before he had examined it properly and had got it safely into the hands of the right authorities, who would realize its tremendous importance; no policeman was going to get his hands on *this*. With a strong twinge of guilt he stowed the fragment in his notebook and reentered the cave to replace the now-innocent hairpiece on the body. When the contingent arrived, headed by Tahir, Toby was back propped against the boulder and puffing on his pipe.

Tahir, who had the look of a much-tried man, was followed by a chunky young police officer and two constables, one of whom carried a canvas stretcher. As he came up, he murmured to Toby in Turkish, "I don't think you are going to enjoy this. The young man behind me is not a good listener and is a man of many prejudices and little judgment. I would not say much. He speaks little English."

The officer shouldered Tahir aside and stepped in front of him. He was square-faced, fair-haired and blue-eyed, and Toby immediately surmised a Germanic-Jewish origin. The blue eyes, small and cold, fixed with heavy suspicion on Toby as the young man rattled off a long sentence at him.

"He asks if you have identification papers on you," Tahir translated.

"*Sprechen-sie Deutsch?*" Toby said hopefully.

The young man looked a little surprised. "*Ja. Officer Haime Baum.*" He continued in German, "But this man said you were British. Identify yourself, please."

"I am British," Toby said with heavy patience in German, "but since I speak no Hebrew and you no English, don't you think it would be better if we communicated in a language we both know? My name is Sir Tobias Glendower, and I am an archaeologist. My papers are all back in the British archaeological expedition camp at Wadi Mugharid and are quite in order—"

"They should be carried with you at all times," Baum interjected.

"I came out here to find the leader of that expedition, Dr. William Pierson," Toby continued, ignoring him, "and have found him—murdered. There are several things in the cave I would like to draw your attention to before you start your investigation —"

"This man says he moved the body," Baum interrupted again, thin-lipped with disapproval, "so you probably have destroyed any worthwhile evidence already. I am quite capable of drawing my own conclusions." He motioned to the two constables, who tramped into the cave. "The main thing is that you can establish the identity of the body. You verify that it is that of this Dr. Pierson?"

"I do."

"Then you may safely leave the rest to us." With a curt nod Baum went in after his assistants.

Tahir looked at Toby and shrugged helplessly. "What did I tell you? The way he went on at the police post, you would have thought I was the murderer. Now, luckily, he has changed his mind."

Toby snorted. "Well, let us hope the case is handed to some higher, more competent authority. He hasn't even brought any equipment, by the looks of it. I won't waste my time trying to point things out to this one. I'll wait to tell my findings in Jerusalem."

"You found something?" Tahir said quickly.

"Oh, a few indications." Toby was vague. "I only hope they have a competent man for the autopsy."

Baum emerged, looking a shade or two paler. "Very bad," he said thickly, "but never fear, we will get those Bedouin devils for this. I have said all along they should be chased right out of the West Bank, and this may persuade the people in Jerusalem to do something about it."

Toby shot a sharp glance at Tahir, who was looking

resigned. "But it is highly unlikely that they are involved in the murder! Let me point out ..."

"They would cut their own mothers' throats for a single *agora*," Baum continued inexorably, "but this time we will get them. They'll die for this. Mind you, foreigners have no business wandering around in the wilderness by themselves. If they ask for trouble like that, it is small wonder that bad things happen. What was this man doing out here anyway all by himself?"

It was Toby's turn to ignore the question. "Well, since you have already solved this case to your satisfaction," he said, "there does not seem much point in discussing it. I take it we may leave? What plans do you have for Dr. Pierson's body?"

Baum cast an uneasy glance at the landscape, which, with the fading sun, was turning from gold to silver-gray. "Yes, you had better go quickly back to your camp; it will be dark soon. But you will have to make a full statement to the people in Jerusalem, tomorrow if possible. We will remove the body to Engedi overnight and take it in the morning to Jerusalem, where the autopsy will be performed. . . ." He scribbled an address on a piece of paper and added his initials. "You will report here in Jerusalem. A policeman from Engedi will pick you up at the camp and guide you. And please bring your papers with you. You had better go at once, since the Bedouin may still be around and I cannot spare a man to guard you back to your camp. We have much work to do here."

Tahir started down the darkening path, but Toby was determined to get in one last word. "The second fissure in the cave was where Dr. Pierson was tortured," he said firmly. "I believe from the nature of the scars he was burned by either cigarettes or a cigar—ashes from these are mixed in with the earth of the floor. Be sure and take samples." And before Baum could say a word, Toby gave a condescending nod and set off after Tahir.

"What did you do with young Dyke?" he inquired as they bumped off slowly back toward the camp.

Tahir's body was slack now with weariness, and his bearded face was grim and lined. "There is a small kibbutz at the oasis. I left him there and said we'd get him tomorrow," he said briefly. "He was still very upset. I did not think you would want him around."

"No." Toby peered into the fast-gathering darkness. "It is vitally important that you say nothing of what has happened today. Time enough for that when the police turn up tomorrow at camp. Keep a sharp eye on everyone for anything at all out of the ordinary. We will say that Robert had a slight accident. I want you to watch everyone's reactions."

"You think then it was somebody at the camp." Tahir's tone was as grim as his face.

"I just don't know. For all I know at the moment, it may be someone we have not even seen or heard of." Toby sighed. "But I think it is a lot more likely to be someone connected with Bill than Baum's theory on the Bedouin."

Tahir grunted, and the rest of the seemingly endless journey passed in silence. After the darkness of the desert, the lights of the little camp seemed almost festive in their brightness as the Jeep rolled to a final stop.

Their coming had evidently been watched for, since Hedecai Schmidt immediately came running from her tent and other tent flaps were pulled back, adding new streams of light to illuminate the latecomers. "Did you find anything . . . ?" Hedecai started eagerly, then her expression changed to one of alarm as she missed the third figure. "Where's Robert?"

Myron Goldsmith had joined her, with Ali-Muhammed close behind and Selwyn Grayson's tall figure bringing up the rear. Toby turned tired eyes on the small group. "We had a misadventure. Robert did some cliff climbing and got shaken up. Nothing serious, but we left him at a kibbutz in Engedi overnight." Which was the literal truth so far as it went. "He should be all right by tomorrow and we can pick him up then."

"Oh, marvelous!" Myron snarled sarcastically. "Not only do you take my foreman for a whole working day, but now you put one of my few able-bodied diggers out of action! And all for nothing, I take it? Well, I can tell you right now, Tahir stays here tomorrow whether you like it or not."

Toby merely shook his head wearily and climbed out.

"I'll go with you in the morning," Ali-Muhammed volunteered quickly, and Selwyn Grayson chimed in, "I'll come along, too. In fact we'll take my Land Rover. It doesn't shake you up as much as the Jeep. You look all in, Professor."

Toby digested the fact that Grayson was puffing on a twisty black Italian cheroot before replying. "Yes, I am tired," he agreed. "So is Tahir, who has been a great help." He placed his hand on the big man's arm and gave it a warning squeeze. "I think we both need a good night's rest, and tomorrow I must go to Jerusalem to check in with Mrs. Pierson and Dr. Spring. But thanks for your offers."

"Dinner is almost ready. You must be hungry after such a long day, and you can tell us over it where you went and what happened," Ali-Muhammed said, and there was an anxious note in his voice.

After all he had been through, the very thought of food revolted Toby, but he was determined they should not suspect how upset he really was. "No, I think I'll pass it up for tonight. Heat got to me a bit, I think." He appealed directly to Hedecai, who was still staring worriedly at him. "Perhaps if you could bring some fruit and that bottle of Scotch to my tent? I'll just have a nightcap, read a bit and then turn right in. Probably will get off early tomorrow."

"Oh, certainly, Professor." And she hurried off toward the mess tent as Toby turned toward his.

"Oh, by the way, Prof," Selwyn said in his nasal drawl, "I understand from Ali that you suggested digging under the face of the cliff, and they hit the biggest find this far—another hidden cistern. I see you have not lost the old touch."

"That's good," Toby said absently and went on his way.

He slumped down on his cot and felt for his notebook with its precious contents. His fingers itched with impatience to examine it further, but he had to steel himself to wait until he could be certain of no interruptions.

Hedecai presently poked her head around the tent flap and the solid rest of her followed, bearing a wooden finds tray laden with the Scotch, a jug of water, a glass and a bowl of oranges, dried figs and nuts. "Is this all right?" she asked anxiously. "I can easily bring you something else as well. Cheese? Biscuits?"

"No, that's very nice. Thank you very much."

She set the tray down on the footlocker and turned to him. "Robert really is all right?"

"Oh, yes, just shaken up, that's all," Toby assured her with as much patience as he could muster. "Nothing sprained or broken."

Her dark eyes searched his. "There's something else, isn't there? Something you aren't telling?"

Damn women's intuition, Toby thought irritably, they'll do it to you every time. "Well, we had a bit of a run-in with some Bedouin," he temporized. "Nothing serious. I expect Robert will want to tell you all about it himself tomorrow." He decided to sidetrack. "What about this new find you made today? Tell me about it." He poured himself a double shot of Scotch and downed it in a couple of gulps.

Hedecai brightened. "Oh, yes, that was really something! It looks like a ritual ablution cistern with steps down to it and everything, just like the one at Qumran. This place must have been more important than we thought." She giggled suddenly. "Myron didn't know whether to be delighted or furious. It's the first decent thing we've found, but he couldn't get over the fact that you took one look at the site and picked it right out. It has kept him muttering to himself all day."

Toby poured another double shot and took a gulp. He was beginning to feel a whole lot better. "Glad to have done something useful, but you'd better run along or your own dinner will be getting cold. Thank you very much for this."

"You're very welcome, Professor. You have no idea how nice it is to have someone who's efficient about this place," Hedecai said with a sudden grin and went out.

Toby waited until her footsteps had died away, then secured the tent flap tightly and placed one of the footlockers and the light on the camp cot. He got out the notebook and extracted the piece of vellum with reverence. Smoothing it out, he got out his pocket magnifier and began to examine it systematically.

The left-hand column was in Hebrew, or possibly Aramaic characters and was beyond him, so he concentrated on the right-hand side, which, by its very formation, was a list of some kind. Laboriously he made out the dark ink letter by letter, transcribing as he went.

MUNITAS ESSENAE. ANNO. III. IMP. TIBERIO. read the incomplete first line. *"Munitas,"* Toby murmured. "Possibly *communitas,* so 'community of the Essenes.' Now, let me see, Year 3 of the Emperor Tiberius would be A.D. 17." Below that there were just three words spaced at intervals across the scroll. AET. NATUS and L. CIVITAS. *"Aet.* for *aetate,* 'aged,' " Toby breathed. *"Natus,* 'born,' *l. civitas,* 'place of residence.' It's a census! It's a census of the Essene community in A.D. 17."

His excitement coupled with the drinks he had downed made him feel quite giddy. To calm himself and clear his head, he tore himself away from his labors long enough to eat a couple of oranges and a handful of figs, and this time added some water to the Scotch in his glass. His head cleared. To make certain it stayed that way, he swallowed a couple of aspirins before getting back to his task. He worked steadily for a while and then sat back and looked again in disbelief at the list in his hand.

The Latin transcription and his translation of it ran:

EZRA FILIUS JACOBUS — Ezra son of Jacob, aged 19. Born Hebron, resident the same.

SIMEON FILIUS ISAAC — Simeon son of Isaac, 24, born Ramla, resident the same.

JOSEPHUS FILIUS ABRAHAM — Joseph son of Abraham, 31, born Jerusalem, resident Arimathea.

JESUS FILIUS JOSEPHUS — Jesus son of Joseph, 24, born Bethlehem, resident Nazareth.

DANIEL FILIUS ZADEK — Daniel son of Zadek, 17, born Megiddo, resident the same.

JUDAS, PATER IGNOTUS — Judas, father unknown, 20, called Iscariot or man of Cario.

Joseph of Arimathea, Jesus of Nazareth and Judas Iscariot—three of the main participants in the drama of the Passion—together here as members of the Essene community nine years before the final tragedy!

Toby sat back limply. If the document before him was

genuine, it would be the archaeological discovery of the century—no, of all time! The first tangible proof outside of the Gospels themselves that Jesus of Bethlehem had really existed! Moreover, it was the type of proof that would be hard to gainsay, for this was no piece of sacred writing, no early scrap of Christian propaganda—this was a prosaic government document; this was a census, so beloved by the bureaucratic Romans, so hated by the Jews.

He knew well that there had been endless speculation that Jesus must have been in contact with the Essenes, since His sayings in the Gospels were so closely linked with many of their teachings; just as there had been endless speculation about where Jesus had been between His visit to Jerusalem as a twelve-year-old boy and when He reappeared for those brief three years of His public ministry. At least in A.D. 17, the young Jesus had been here, together with the man who buried him and the man who betrayed him. The implications exploded in Toby's mind like firecrackers.

One thing he knew for sure, overriding everything else; he must get this precious scrap to Jerusalem and into safe hands, where it could be verified and dated before its marvelous content could be released to a doubting world. And underlying all his thought was a feeling of great joy. Bill had died protecting this vital thing, but he had not died in vain. In his death he had achieved what had eluded him all his life—he had made the greatest archaeological discovery of them all and would reap undying fame; he, Tobias Glendower, would see to that . . .

In his overtired, overwrought state, his emotions got the better of him and tears pricked his eyes. "God bless you, Bill," he muttered brokenly, and then sudden terror seized him lest something should happen to him or the document before he could get it to safety. He felt the tiny island of the tent surrounded by watchful eyes, the focus of hostile forces. Where could he hide it, protect it? He must go. He must go at once to Jerusalem.

A sound from the night fanned his terror as over the moaning of the night wind came the spluttering roar of an engine. A vehicle was laboring up the steep incline to the camp plateau from the plain below. He glanced at his watch and saw it was almost midnight. "Who the devil . . . !"

With hands that shook he carefully refolded the vellum and, dumping the contents of most of a tin of tobacco into his pouch, hid the folded fragment under the remainder.

The unknown vehicle coughed to a stop, and Toby could hear stirrings about the camp. He buried the tobacco tin back among his gear and, undoing the tent flap, stepped out into the chill of the night. A small camper, much battered and bemired, was drawn up at the very edge of the plateau, its lights still on. By them he could make out the outlines of two people: a large, shaggy-haired man and a small woman with long, dark hair.

A bass voice boomed out of the darkness. "Who is in charge here?"

Toby could see Ali and Hedecai, and Selwyn's head came popping out through the opening of the orange tent. There was no sign of Myron. Toby stepped forward. "I am Sir Tobias Glendower," he boomed back. "And who might you be?"

The large figure shambled toward him and smiled through a fuzzy beard, revealing a gold tooth in the front of his mouth. "My name is Gregory Vadik, and this is my wife, Vashti. The spirits have spoken and have sent us. We have come to aid you. By our psychic powers we will help you locate your missing leader, William Pierson. He calls to us from the wilderness!"

CHAPTER 9

"Tahir, wake up!" Toby shook the shoulder of the sleeping man with the roughness of anxiety. "I have to go to Jerusalem right now. I can't wait for the policeman from Engedi. When he comes, tell him I will meet him at the police headquarters in Jerusalem at the appointed time. Do you understand what I am saying?"

The big Kurd stirred, got up on one elbow and regarded him blearily. "What is the matter, *effendi?* What has happened?"

"It's just some business I have to take care of, and I want no trouble with the police. Will you do what I ask?"

"*Evet, effendi,*" Tahir murmured with a huge yawn and, slumping down, was instantly asleep again.

Toby had snatched a couple of restless hours of sleep himself, but this latest development, coming on top of everything else, had disquieted him even more. Was the arrival of the Vadiks as fortuitous and as crackbrained as it appeared, or was it a lot more significant than that? Had faces now been put on his unknown factor—X—and, if so, what were they after? This thought had kept him tossing on the narrow cot, and with the earliest light of dawn he had decided that his first priority must be the safeguarding of the Jesus document and that he must leave right away.

He crept back through the sleeping camp to his tent, salvaged the document from its unusual hiding place and, as quietly as he could, negotiated his own Jeep past the Vadik camper, which, with its presumably sleeping occupants, partially blocked the trail off the plateau. Not until he was on the track below leading to the main Jericho–Engedi road did he open the throttle and speed off beside the deceptively calm morning face of the Dead Sea. He sped past the quiet ruins of Qumran, high on their own plateau to his left, then on through the still-sleeping town

85

of Jericho, and began the long, twisting haul up the steep escarpment that led to the Holy City.

Jerusalem, golden on its hills in the morning sun, was already stirring into busy life as he bore off from the Jericho Road to the Nablus Road, making his way directly toward the British School of Archaeology. There, just as Penny had been the day before, he was baffled: A sleepy and startled servant informed him that there was no one there except the assistant librarian and some students. Toby, silently fuming, threw himself back into the Jeep and headed for the American school. Here his luck was better, and after some preliminary skirmishing he was allowed entrance to the assistant director.

Garth Edwards, who had breakfasted early in order to get what he hoped would be a long and uninterrupted session with his fascinating papyrus, was more than a little startled when his door burst open and a tall, stooped man, his unshaved face gray with stubble and fatigue, his blazing blue eyes red-rimmed with weariness, swooped down upon him.

"Dr. Edwards from the Princeton Theological Seminary?" the apparition barked. "I am Sir Tobias Glendower, professor of archaeology at the University of Oxford, and I have most urgent need of your expertise and of the facilities of the American school."

Only the name, which was familiar to him, prevented Garth Edwards from leaping from his chair and running for safety as the apparent madman towered over him. As it was, he flattened himself back in his chair and said faintly, "Oh! Sir Tobias Glendower—of course. Er—what can I do for you?"

"Well, first I would like you to make a transcript of the Aramaic or Hebrew in this, to see if it equates with my transcription of the Latin. Then I would like to make some photographic prints of it—I know you have the facilities here. And after that I'd like you to come with me as a witness when I hand the document over to an old acquaintance of mine, Dr. Maisler, at the Archaeological Museum. You will see why when you have read it." Toby took out the folded scroll scrap and laid it carefully on top of Edwards's own precious manuscript. "It is a matter of the utmost urgency," he trumpeted on, "and there is no time to waste since I have to be at police headquarters by ten."

"Police headquarters?" Garth echoed faintly, more convinced than ever that he was facing a madman. "May I ask what . . . ?"

"I have to make a statement concerning the murder of Dr. William Pierson, the discoverer of this document," Toby broke in impatiently, "so, for heaven's sake, get on with it, man!"

"Murder! Good heavens!" Edwards mumbled, and lapsed into silence as his eyes strayed over the scroll. Suddenly he sucked in his breath, his eyes widened, and after an amazed stare at Toby he took up his pen and began to write furiously. Toby took out the Latin transcript and quietly laid it on the desk by his elbow. In a short space of time Edwards had finished his list, and his eyes glazed with wonder as he compared his transcript with Toby's. Then he mutely handed them both to Toby. "Can it possibly be genuine?" he muttered excitedly.

Toby cast a rapid eye over the Aramaic transcript. *Ezra bar Jacob, Simeon bar Isaac, Joseph bar Abraham, Jeshua bar Joseph, Daniel bar Zadek, Judas Iscariot.* "Ah, of course! Jeshua being the correct form of Jesus," he muttered, "and otherwise exactly as the Latin." Then looking up at the thunderstruck Garth Edwards, "Its authenticity will have to be tested, of course. I don't suppose you have any C-14 dating facilities here?"

"No, we have to send back to the States or get it done here by the Israelis," Garth said dazedly, "but if this is genuine—my God!"

"Quite. So you see why we had better make copies of it without further delay," Toby said. He was beginning to enjoy his new partner, who was evidently a man of few words and quick perception.

"This way." The big, freckled face of Garth Edwards was solemn now with determination. "I expect you do not want anyone else in on this, so I'll do it myself. Our photographer is not here at the moment, but I think I can manage." He led the way down to the small photography lab in the basement.

Within half an hour they had made copies of the document by every conceivable means in the well-stocked laboratory of the school, including some Polaroid shots which determined immediately that the writing on the aged vellum was remarkably distinct and readable. "I don't suppose," Garth said wistfully, "we dare take a sample of the scroll for our own C-14 lab back home?"

Toby hesitated. "We dare not take the large sample it would require. It would be tantamount to mutilating the manuscript, which could lead to all sorts of later problems."

"This new ion-count refinement of the C-14 process only requires a very minute sample and is every bit as accurate in the time range we will be dealing with," Garth tempted. "It would at least give us some countercheck. After all, this is not going to sit too well with some sections of the Jewish community."

They looked at one another in silence for a moment, then said in unison, "Let's do it." They carefully detached a scrap of the ragged bottom edge that was bare of writing and sealed it in a glassine packet. As an afterthought Toby fished in his pocket for the envelope and extracted the scrap he had found in the murder cave. "While we are about it we may as well have this done, too." He did not elaborate but removed the fragment and sealed it in another envelope. "How quickly do you think you can get the information?"

Garth wrinkled his freckled brow. "There's a colleague returning to the States today. I'll give them to him and make sure they are given top priority at the lab. I'll ask the man I know there to call me as soon as the results are known. Say about a week."

"Good. Now let's get off to Maisler—though I am not at all sure how he is going to react to having this dumped in his lap."

"He will probably be as thunderstruck as I am," Garth confessed, and hurried after Toby down to the Jeep.

Abe Maisler, who looked like a miniature copy of Albert Einstein even to the bushy hair and lugubrious mustache, was evidently most disconcerted as the two excited men crowded into his small, cluttered office at the Archaeological Museum, one flourishing an antique document and the other with two rather worn-looking bits of paper. He could scarcely believe that the blazing-eyed scarecrow of a man who was disjointedly gabbling his incredible story was the same man he had last seen in his rather pontifical and extremely British calm presiding at an international conference.

The contents of the document, however, had their usual effect. After he had studied it and the transcripts, his face tightened and hardened and he said flatly, "How did this come into your possession, Sir Tobias? To the best of my knowledge you have no excavating or archaeological permit for this country."

"*I* did not find it. It was discovered by Dr. William Pierson of the British archaeological expedition at Wadi Mugharid, who safeguarded this discovery with his very life. He has been murdered—tortured and murdered. I found it concealed on his body." Toby's voice faltered momentarily, then grew stronger. "As to where he found it, I have no clear idea, but it is just possible that the find spot was the cave in which he was subsequently murdered." He extracted the remaining scrap of vellum from his pocket and laid it beside the other. "I found a broken scroll pot in the cave and this scrap with it. Carbon-14 dating should verify the dates on both and their authenticity."

"Naturally that will be the very first step, and until it is done it would be in everyone's interest, I think, that there be absolutely no publicity." Maisler's tone was frosty. "And what is Dr. Edwards's role in this, may I ask?"

"I am no Hebrew scholar. I needed Dr. Edwards's expertise to establish that this was not just some clumsy forgery. He also agreed to accompany me here to witness the handing over of the scroll fragment, a document of such potential vital importance."

"Which does not say a great deal for your opinion of me, either as a scientist of integrity or as a scholar," Maisler said dryly, but something like a twinkle appeared in the dark eyes under the bushy gray eyebrows. "However, you were perfectly and understandably correct. I am well aware of what importance this document will have, if it is genuine, to the Christian world. I am also well aware that it will not be gladly received by certain circles of my own people." He gave a light sigh. "In fact this is quite a bombshell you have dumped in my lap. Secrecy is extremely important at this juncture, and yet *how* it is to be kept secret if a man has been murdered for it is difficult to see."

Toby took refuge in pomposity. "I have reason to believe that Dr. Pierson's murder was not connected directly with this document," he said slowly. "I am afraid at this point I cannot give reasons for my belief, but since we are all agreed on the need for secrecy, I must ask both of you to have faith in me for the moment and to keep the existence of this document a secret among the three of us. I fully intend to discover the identity of Dr. Pierson's murderer and will bend every effort to assist the Israeli police in their investigations, but unless I am convinced that this figures in the case, I would prefer to cloak its existence, at least until the C-14 test is made. Do you agree to this, Dr. Maisler?"

The little scientist looked at him curiously. "To the secrecy, yes. But why do you think the murder is unconnected with the discovery?"

Toby shook his head. "I am afraid as of now I can give you no valid reasons, but I have had a certain amount of experience in these matters, and you will just have to trust my judgment. I can only say at present that there do seem to be other factors and motives involved."

Maisler shrugged resignedly. "Well, that is between you and the police." He scribbled something on a piece of paper and handed it to Toby. "Your receipt," he said with a faint grin. It read, "Received from Sir Tobias Glendower, one unidentified scroll scrap said to be from the Wilderness of Judea and found by Dr. William Pierson, deceased," followed by the date and his signature. "So far as I am concerned, that is as far as it goes at the present. I suppose I ought to be grateful that it was not spirited away to America, where it would have had to be ransomed by us for untold wealth, but in this case I almost wish it had been." He grinned slyly at both of them. "Unless, of course, it *is* a fake. Either way I will let you know. Good day, gentlemen."

"Of all the nerve!" Garth Edwards exploded when they were outside. "The greatest find of the century and all he could do was make snide wisecracks."

"Well, you can scarcely blame him," Toby said wearily. "After all the trouble and commotion between America and Israel over the Dead Sea Scrolls, I suppose he's entitled to a cheap shot or two." He looked at his watch and groaned softly. "I have to get over to the police HQ. Will you let me know immediately when the C-14 lab report gets in from the States?"

"Of course—but where and how do I get in touch?" Garth asked eagerly. "What are your plans?"

"As soon as I'm through here, I'll be going back to Wadi Mugharid. Short of coming down yourself, I don't see how we can make direct contact. But you could pass the word to a colleague of mine who is staying at the Sheikh Jarrah Hotel, Dr. Penelope Spring."

"Spring, Spring?" Garth wrinkled his brows. "Now where have I heard that name? Oh yes, yesterday! She came to see me."

"What on earth for?"

"Trying to locate an old American friend of hers, she said. Now let me see, who was it? Ah! A Selwyn Grayson. I'm afraid I couldn't help her. Never set eyes on the man."

Now what was Penny up to or onto, Toby thought, as Garth continued, "But I thought this was to be kept strictly between us."

"Oh, you can tell *her;* we're partners," Toby said testily. "If we are going to clear this matter up, she's got to be in on it, too. Teamwork, that's what crime solving is, teamwork," and he hurried off to his rendezvous with the police.

Even in his tense state he was soothed by his interview with the inspector to whom he had been directed by the extremely nervous young Engedi constable he had found pacing up and down in front of the central police headquarters. Inspector Abrams, whose gray hair belied his youthful face, was an amiable man with keen, intelligent brown eyes. He spoke excellent English and was a pipe smoker, which immediately warmed Toby's heart to him. He gently led Toby through the identification and his statement and at the end of it sat back in his leather chair, lit up his pipe and, after a few satisfied puffs, asked casually, "So what do you make of this nasty business, Sir Tobias?"

"Well, your own man at Engedi seems to be fixed on the

idea of the Bedouin as culprits," Toby said irritably, "but I do not think it is that simple." He detailed his find of the heel print and handed over the envelope containing the ash from the torture chamber. "By the look of the burn scars it seemed to me that they were made by a cigarette or cigar. I suppose Bedouin *do* smoke sometimes, but I've never seen one do so. And the whole set-up looked to me like a one-man operation."

"Yes, but to what purpose?" Abrams said mildly. "And he *was* robbed, you know. No wallet, watch or anything like that found on the body."

Toby had no answer. Instead he said, "If the motive were merely robbery, why do that to him? It looks more like revenge or hate, and for those there are stronger motives nearer to home. I would be most obliged if you would let me have the autopsy findings."

"Oh, stronger motives, you say?" Abrams's eyebrows raised. "Such as?"

Toby felt uncomfortable but felt it had to be done. "Professional jealousy, for one. Ours is a strange profession, Inspector, and a very competitive one. Bill Pierson's arch-rival, Selwyn Grayson, turned up unexpectedly at the site just after Bill's disappearance and is still there, for reasons totally obscure. Then Bill's assistant, Myron Goldsmith, was not on the best of terms with him, and his Arab assistant, Ali-Muhammed, has been behaving in a rather odd fashion."

"Oh yes, we know a thing or two about him," Abrams murmured. "An Iraqi but possibly a PLO man—were you aware of that?"

"No, I wasn't," Toby said shortly, "but there you have another possible motive. Bill would never have stood for that, I know. And there is also the possibility that a complete outsider is involved. Someone, perhaps, who thought Bill had found something valuable and was after it. Tell me, do you know anything about a Gregory Vadik?"

Abrams stiffened. "Gregory Vadik? Why do you ask?"

"Because he and his wife turned up at the site late last night offering to help find Dr. Pierson by their 'psychic' powers," Toby replied. "And I was unable to discover how they even knew he was missing."

"I know of Gregory Vadik," Abrams said, and for a

moment his face aged to match his gray hairs, "but I did not know he was back in Israel. His wife, Vashti, has a considerable reputation as a medium. I do not put much store in such things myself, although I suppose I should not say that with a fellow countryman like Uri Geller." He smiled faintly, but there was no amusement in the dark eyes. "In any case the Vadiks need not concern you. In fact my advice to you is to keep well away from this business. Unfortunately, I cannot allow you to leave Israel just yet, but from now on this is a police matter. Leave everything to us."

Toby was not about to antagonize him by stating his own iron resolve, so he temporized. "I will, of course, have to break the news to Mrs. Pierson. Then I feel I should return to the site to finish up and close down the excavation. I doubt in these circumstances whether anyone will wish to continue."

Abrams nodded but looked at him searchingly. "Well, so long as that is *all* you do. I repeat, do not concern yourself with this. We will get to the bottom of it, I assure you. And a word of warning to you: wherever the Vadiks are, things happen. And Gregory Vadik is strictly bad news."

CHAPTER 10

Penny was feeling extremely excited and pleased with herself. She had garnered such a store of information in the past forty-eight hours that she felt if she did not pass it on to Toby soon, she would probably burst. In spite of all his injunctions to the contrary, she was seriously considering hiring a car and driving down to the site, but was currently wondering how she could achieve this and also tactfully evade her employer, who had been dogging her footsteps all morning. She had managed to disengage herself for the moment with the excuse that she had an important business letter to write.

Hurrying back to the temporary refuge of her room, Penny was waylaid by a frightened-looking maid clutching an armful of towels. She grabbed at Penny's arm and said in broken English, "No go. Man in room." She flourished a towel. "Want to put. Man . . ." She closed her eyes and made a snoring sound. "Get police?"

"Good heavens! A man . . ." A sudden thought occurred to Penny and she shook her head. "No police. I look. Come!" With the maid panting excitedly behind her, she poked her head cautiously around the door. Curled up like a giant baby on the bed, Sir Tobias Glendower lay in all his glory snoring up a mild hurricane. Penny turned to the horrified maid and grinned. "No police." She put her fingers to her lips. "Friend. All right." The maid gave a relieved sigh, grinned knowingly at her and tiptoed away.

Penny went in and quietly closed the door. She crossed over and looked down at her oblivious partner with a mixture of exasperation and affection. "Well, you do look as if you've been through the mill!" she muttered. A note propped up against the small, hazy mirror on the dressing table caught her eye. In Toby's neat handwriting it read:

The worst has happened. Bill is dead. Murdered. Will you break the news to Valerie before the police ar-

rive? Too exhausted to face it. Will fill you in later.
P.S. If I'm asleep, don't wake me.

"Gee, thanks a whole heap for this merry little chore!"
Penny cast a reproachful glance at the bed. "And a fat lot
of information you've given *me* to pass on, I must say.
What were you trying to do, win a twenty-five-words-or-less
contest?"

Toby gobbled in his sleep and buried deeper into the pil-
low. Penny looked at his ravaged, unshaven face. "Forgot
his shaving things again, I see." She rummaged in his case
under the bed, found the required articles, put them in full
view on the dressing table and turning over his note, wrote
on the back:

If you waken before I get back, use these immediately.
You look like a moth-eaten Rip Van Winkle. Thanks
for the brilliantly lucid note, but will do as bidden.

And to make her displeasure abundantly clear, she
signed her full name with a flourish: "Penelope Athene
Spring." She braced herself. "Might as well get it over
with, I suppose," she said and stumped indignantly out to
find the new widow.

Since the little hotel was too humble to have anything
as elegant as a residents' lounge, there was only one place
to look for Valerie—in her room. Penny made her way
there, half hoping that Valerie had departed on yet another
shopping orgy so that she would be spared her unpleasant
task at least for a while.

Her luck was out, and Valerie in. "Finished already?"
Valerie remarked as she opened the door. "I thought you'd
be busy all morning, so I was just going out by myself."

"Something important has come up. I'd better come in
and you'd better sit down." Penny was grim in her ner-
vousness.

Valerie's thin hands fluttered to her mouth and her eyes
widened. "Something about Bill? Has he been found?"

Penny nodded and shut the door behind her. She motioned Valerie to the room's lone chair and perched on
the bed. "There's no easy way to do this," she said, "but
I'm afraid I have bad news for you. Bill is dead."

Valerie sat rigid, her pale face now a chalky white. "Not suicide?" she whispered.

It jolted Penny, but she managed to conceal it. "No, worse than that, I'm afraid. He was found murdered."

"But where . . . how . . . ?" Valerie was scarcely audible. "How do you know?"

"I had word from Toby," Penny said, carefully omitting the fact that he was in the hotel. "He wanted me to break the news before the police arrived."

"Police?" Valerie seemed dazed.

"Well, of course the Israeli authorities will be investigating his death," Penny said with a hint of impatience. "You'll have to decide what you are going to tell them when they do come. I know no details, so until we do know more, I would suggest saying as little as possible."

Valerie drew herself together. "Naturally!" she said frostily. "I'm not a complete fool, you know!" Then, belatedly, "Poor Bill!"

So much for the anguished grief of the bereaved, thought Penny. Epitaph for a dead, unloved husband. Oh well, it figures, I suppose. Then she came to the grim realization that she would have to be the bearer of ill tidings to another woman in the city, to whom it would bring a greater grief. "Would you like me to stay or would you prefer to be alone?" she said aloud. "Can I get you anything. A drink? I have some brandy in my room. I know this has been a terrible shock."

"No, I'm all right," Valerie said and got up. "I must make some telephone calls to London, though how one does so from this wretched little hotel . . ."

Heavy boots tramped down the corridor and there was a knock on the door. Penny opened it to find the startled-looking manager with a gray-haired, young-faced man in police uniform behind him. "The police to see you, Mrs. Pierson," the manager muttered uneasily.

The policeman came in, giving Penny a curious glance in passing, and went over to Valerie. "Inspector Abrams, Mrs. Pierson, of the Jerusalem police. Have you seen Sir Tobias Glendower yet?"

She shook her head. "Then I am afraid I have some ill tidings for you. Would you care to sit down?"

Valerie stood tense, looking at him. "If it is about my

husband, Dr. Spring has just informed me of his death," she answered, indicating Penny.

Abrams swung quickly around. "How did you know?" he demanded.

"A message from Sir Tobias," Penny said guiltily. "He asked me to break the news."

He looked searchingly at her, then gave a dismissive nod. "I see. Well, if you will excuse us?"

Penny would dearly have loved to hang around to hear more of the details, but could think of no graceful way of doing so. She looked warningly at the stone-faced Valerie and said, "I'll be in my room if you need me," and went out with manifest reluctance.

Toby was still wrapped in noisy slumber, so after a few minutes she decided she might as well get her second unpleasant task over with and so took a cab to the British School. Here her good intentions were thwarted. Miss Cochran, she was informed, was sick and would not be in today. "It's important I get in touch with her," Penny pleaded. "Will you give me her home address, or at least her phone number?"

Miss Cochran had no phone and they were sorry but they could not give out home addresses; if she cared to leave a message, they would see it was delivered to Miss Cochran. Baffled, Penny scribbled a note asking Margaret Cochran to get in touch with her immediately at the hotel and retreated.

When she got back to the little whitewashed front of the hotel, she saw that the police car had gone. On entering the lobby she found Valerie, her back turned to the entrance, talking into the phone at the registration desk. She was speaking loudly and clearly, and it was evident that the connection was bad because she kept saying, "What?" and, "Repeat that, please," with mounting degrees of impatience. Finally she almost shouted into the phone, "As soon as I get the death certificate, I'll send it. And I expect your company to make good on its obligations *at once,* is that clear? If there is any quibbling on your part, I shall instruct my lawyer to sue immediately, *do you understand?*" She slammed the phone down with a hand that trembled and swung around toward the stairs. When she saw Penny standing there, an ugly flush mounted her drawn cheeks and her eyes narrowed. "And how long have you been eavesdropping?" she demanded viciously.

Penny looked at her with bland, innocent hazel eyes. "I've just come in, but since this is so public a place and you were talking so loudly, I should hardly call it eavesdropping. One of your London calls, I presume?" Then she added silkily, "To your insurance agent, Mr. Doyle?"

Valerie wilted visibly. "How did you know?" she gasped.

Penny was on the point of saying, "We have our methods, my dear Watson," but realized this was no time to be flippant. Instead she said reasonably, "I know you are upset, but you will have to be a little patient. I'm afraid in a case of murder the insurance company will be within its rights to withhold payment, pending the outcome of the investigation. It's just standard procedure."

"But that's so unfair!" Sudden tears spilled out of the pale blue eyes. "Bill took that policy out expressly for *me*. He said he wanted to pay me back for all the money I had spent on him over the years, and that if this venture failed at least I'd have that insurance eventually. And I *need* it." This was almost a wail.

Either Valerie was unbelievably money hungry or Penny's original hunch had been right and the fortune was gone; Penny was inclined to believe the latter. "It was for a large amount?" she asked casually.

Valerie drew herself up, brushing away the tears with a trembling hand. "I do not think that is any of your business, Dr. Spring. And furthermore, I shall have no more need of your services; not that, as far as I can see, you have *done* anything. But as of now I am officially terminating our rather ridiculous agreement." She turned on her heel and stamped up the stairs.

"Well, the sooner the murder is cleared up, the sooner you'll get your money," Penny said softly to the retreating figure. "That is, if you are not involved."

She went up to her own room and listened at the door. There was no sound of snoring, so she went in. Toby was sitting on the edge of the bed, his hands on his knees, gazing dazedly out the window. At her entrance, he looked up and announced lugubriously, "Oh, it's you—I feel terrible."

"You look worse than terrible." She got the brandy bottle and poured him a shot. "Drink that and then be my guest." She waved a hand at the washbasin. "You can tell me all about it while you shave. Currently you look like the wrath of God."

"Have you seen Valerie?"

"Yes, and she just fired me from the case. The grieving widow seems to be more interested in collecting the insurance than in finding out who murdered her husband. And thanks for that dandy little chore! Now suppose you tell me what it is all about."

Toby gave a relieved sigh and started to gather up his shaving things. "On top of everything else, that was one thing I just could not face. Just wait till you hear . . ." And to the accompaniment of much splashing and scraping, he took her step by step through the grisly events of his sojourn in the wilderness.

Penny heard him out in silence. When he had finished, she handed him another drink. "Pretty awful," she commented. "No wonder you're all in. I'm sorry, Toby. I know how fond you were of Bill Pierson. You are going on with it, of course?" He nodded. "You want me in on it?"

He looked at her with deep gloom and tossed down the rest of the drink. "It's nasty and likely to get nastier. I certainly don't want you to come down to the camp, but there may be some things you can do here if you want to stay."

"That's all I wanted to hear." She smiled faintly at him. "I've already picked up quite a bit." And she proceeded to tell him of her successful search for the "other woman" and of Selwyn Grayson's strange activities.

At the end of it, Toby sighed and shook his head perplexedly. "It seems to me we have altogether too many suspects and too many motives. At the moment it is just one big tangle, and I can see no sign of the main thread. The only people on the dig I can firmly rule out are the two students. It's not likely that Tahir and John Carter are involved, but I can't rule them out entirely. And now we have the added puzzle of the Vadiks, whose presence seemed to upset the able Inspector Abrams so. Why, I have no idea."

"I'm afraid you can't take Carter off the hook at all,"

Penny said slowly. "I haven't told you all my news. I have had one big stroke of luck that I haven't had a chance to tell you about yet. Just by chance I ran into an old student of mine in a restaurant where I had dinner last night. She's married to a Foreign Office man who is temporarily here with a British political delegation involved with some sort of dealings with the Knesset—not that that is important. What is important is that I asked her about John Carter on the off chance that she may have heard of him. It seems she had and what she had heard was not good. She said she'd check with her husband, who knows him better, and let me know if there is anything else, but to put it in a nutshell: (a) Carter has been in trouble and very nearly got booted out of the FO several years ago; (b) he is a big spender and is always in financial difficulties; and (c) he has a rather hazy reputation as a Lothario, but that might just be because he is a middle-aged bachelor; and lastly—and this is from my own observation—I'd say he and Valerie Pierson may have a little affair going on the side. Bill's inamorata said as much, too, so it may have been going on for some time."

"What did you think of him?"

"I? I have never seen him."

"Oh!" Toby looked wonderingly at the shaving tackle in his hands. "No, of course these would not be here if you had. I asked him to pick them up for me. Still, it is hard to equate him with this kind of nastiness. He seems such a clean-cut type."

"Appearances aren't much to go by," Penny said wryly, thinking of the two murderers she had dealt with. "Neither of our multiple murderers *looked* the part."

"My own favorite suspect would be Grayson," Toby went on with his own train of thought, "save for one fact that sticks in my gullet—Bill's toupee. His murderer had searched him, had tortured him hideously, and yet had not looked in that very obvious place—indicating clearly that he did not know Bill wore one. This to my mind seems to rule out Grayson, who must have been aware that Bill was already going bald in North Africa."

"*If* they actually met then," Penny put in. "And anyway, isn't that going on the assumption that he was after this

Jesus document of yours? Isn't it more likely that all he was after was the scroll for Zadok's treasure?"

Toby looked pityingly at her. "Any archaeologist would have given an arm and a leg for the Jesus document. To go after a piddling scrap referring to a probably non-existent treasure instead would not make any sense at all."

"But that's just *your* belief," Penny said quickly. "It may not be the murderer's. He may not even have been aware of this new scroll scrap. And don't you think he may have got what he was after and then killed Bill? Find your clue scrap and you may find the murderer. But just suppose you are right about the toupee clue: whom does that leave you with as suspects?"

"Practically everyone," Toby sighed. "Ali-Muhammed had not seen Bill since the old Iraqi days; Goldsmith's only known him since the Liverpool project; Carter since East African days, after Bill had started to wear it. Even Tahir had never worked with him before. Bill got him through one of his colleagues in Liverpool. And, unless the Vadiks are lying, they have never met him at all."

"Which does not get you very far." Penny was matter-of-fact. "So you'll have to try another angle. What are you going to do right now?"

Toby poured himself another drink and tossed it down absentmindedly. "Go back to the dig. Go back to where I found Bill. I've still got to find out what he was doing in that particular spot. That wadi had more vegetation than any other in the area I saw. It just might have been near the supposed location of Zadok's tomb. I'll just have to explore some more. I've also got to find out what the hell the Vadiks are all about. That is about all I can do until I know the results of the autopsy, the ash samples and the result from the C-14 tests on the Jesus scroll."

"So you'll be coming up again? When?"

Toby shook his head. "No, I've told Edwards to give the information to you. Abrams also."

"Then how will you get it from me? Shall I come down?"

He cogitated. "No. I don't want you to get involved unless it is vital. I'll phone you every other day from Jericho or Engedi. If you don't hear from me, you'd better alert Abrams, who strikes me as a very sound man, and come on down to see what has happened."

Penny felt a twinge of unease. "Don't take any chances, will you?" she coaxed. "After all, the police can handle the heavy stuff. As you say, Inspector Abrams struck me as an intelligent man. It's silly to stick your own neck out."

Toby snorted. "That's a fine statement coming from you of all people! As for sticking your neck out, you must be the all-time champion."

"Yes, but I have always had you to come galloping to the rescue," she returned. "I'm not sure I would be as good at it."

"If necessary I'm sure you'll manage." He put on his jacket and put his shaving things in his pocket. "I suppose Valerie will be heading home soon, so that's one less worry you will have."

"I don't know," Penny said slowly. "I'm not so sure about that. In fact I will be very interested to see what our Valerie will do next. She seems to me to be a woman with a very definite object in mind, and I think that object is still Zadok's treasure."

CHAPTER 11

Toby had not been looking forward to his reception at the camp, which his imagination had pictured in varying degrees from icy to actively hostile, but he was totally unprepared for what he did find. As his Jeep breasted the final rise of the dirt track, the small settlement of tents in their orderly rows spread out before him, but of human activity there was no sign at all; nothing stirred, nothing moved. The Vadiks' camper was still there, pulled off close to Grayson's Land Rover, which stood beside his closed tent. The remaining expedition Jeep sat silently near the mess tent, from behind which came the subdued clucking of caged hens. "Anybody here?" he called out, but not a tent flap moved nor a human voice replied.

Feeling a little apprehensive, he went over to Bill's tent with the bagful of supplies he had picked up in Jerusalem. Inside, everything was exactly as he had left it—the cot a rumpled chaos of bedclothes, the tray Hedecai had brought still standing on the footlocker with the dirty glass and empty whiskey bottle. "Where is everybody?" he muttered peevishly as he dumped the duffel bag of supplies on the cot.

He had decided after all to spend the night in Jerusalem, partly to get a good night's sleep and partly because his prodding conscience had dictated he see the widowed Valerie. It had been a most unsatisfactory interview. He had found her cold and withdrawn, and almost totally uninterested in what he had to say. Not that he had had any intention of inflicting the gruesome details of Bill's death on her, but when he had tried to tell her the circumstances of the discovery, she had shut him off with a curt "I really do not feel up to hearing about it. I'd rather not discuss it." Further, when he had tried to find out about the closing of the dig, which he had automatically assumed she would favor, he found her evasive to the point of indifference. "I suppose that will be up to Myron now," she had said. "Obviously he can expect no further funds from me, but so long as he has the London University money to pay the workmen, I suppose he will continue. I gather from Inspector Abrams that no one from the expedition will be allowed to leave Israel until matters are somewhat clearer, so I see no reason why they should not continue the dig. After all, that's what they are here for." This had so shocked him that he had forborne bringing up the question of the treasure. A further shock had been in store when she added, "Since I probably won't be allowed to leave either, I may come down to the dig myself in a day or two."

"Insufferable woman!" he muttered miserably to himself as he looked at a snapshot of her and a clean-shaven Bill taken in earlier, happier days, which was perched on a box by the cot. The small tent suddenly seemed filled with the sense of Bill's presence and he could not bear it a moment longer. "Oh, fifty thousand hells!" he exploded and strode out of it, his face grim with decision, toward the excavation.

Here, and quite irrationally, his sense of outrage increased as he rounded the spur to see the entire complement of the camp quietly and serenely going about its business. He stalked over to the nearest trench and gazed down at what appeared to be a gaily painted mushroom; the mushroom tilted at the sound of his footsteps to reveal the small, startled face of Vashti Vadik under an improbably large sun hat.

"Oh, it's you!" she gasped, and the pupils of her amazing pale green eyes contracted like a cat's as the sun hit them.

"Still here, Mrs. Vadik?" he barked. "That rather surprises me, since I am sure by this time you must have heard the bad news."

She shrank back at the brusqueness of his tone. "Yes, well," she faltered, "you see, the police said no one must leave. And we would like to help in any way we can. . . ."

"You have had previous experience?" Toby trumpeted, as if interviewing a not-too-satisfactory student.

"Why, yes, in my country, in Bulgaria, as a student . . ."

A large shadow fell across her and Toby looked up to see the bulky figure of Gregory Vadik on the other side of the trench. His gold tooth flashed in the sun as he smiled at Toby, but there was no hint of amusement in the deep-set, dark eyes. "Back on the job again, Sir Tobias, eh? I hope you are not criticizing my poor wife for her technique. What she lacks in expertise she makes up for in empathy, believe me. She has picked up that this place was of great learning and serenity, and already there have been results."

"But her powers did not apparently foresee Dr. Pierson's death," Toby said with heavy irony.

Gregory Vadik's smile died. "It is because you do not understand the nature of these powers that you make such a—forgive me—silly statement. She knew there was danger, great danger, but—alas!—this knowledge came too late, and by the time we got here . . ."

"From where?" Toby asked bluntly.

This time the amusement was in his eyes. "We were crossing from Syria to Jordan when the message came to her, so we changed our plans and came directly here. You may get the details from the police, if you wish. We have already told them all of this."

Seeing Myron coming toward them and anticipating a far-from-friendly reception from that quarter, Toby withdrew, feeling that Vadik had definitely taken the honors in that exchange and that he did not wish to lose further ground by a public dressing down from Myron. Again he was surprised.

Goldsmith was more excited than annoyed as their paths intercepted. "At last we have found something worthwhile!" he exclaimed. "It looks as if we have hit a scriptorium." He beckoned Toby excitedly to follow and began to retrace his steps to where Grayson and Ali-Muhammed were crouched in a trench. "Even some scroll fragments are coming out! I don't see how Bill could have missed them. It was where he was digging just before—"

"Scroll fragments!" Toby interrupted sharply. "Over there, and you've let Grayson and Ali . . . ?"

Myron halted abruptly and turned on him. "You must think I'm a complete idiot. They are the most experienced diggers here besides myself. There is no one else I'd trust on this, but I don't take my eyes off either one," he said with quiet venom. "And if I'm not there, Hedecai takes over. But I *am* interested to see that you have noticed the link between the two of them," he added and strode on.

Since the thought had not until that moment occurred to Toby, he followed somewhat subdued. Grayson was busy with trowel and brush on what appeared to be a scribe's bench of smooth-plastered mud brick; at his feet crouched Ali, similarly armed, who was industriously defining the outlines of several scroll pots. Hedecai, ostensibly directing the efforts of the Arab basket boys, was keeping an eagle eye on the trench. As Myron came up, she gave a slight nod and moved off.

Ali looked up, ignoring Toby, and said to Myron, "I'm not certain, but I don't think there is anything *in* the pots. The scraps were lying scattered around the floor as if they'd been torn up."

"Right, then; photograph them as is and then take them out," Myron ordered. He suddenly looked very different from the harassed and insecure man Toby had seen up to this point.

"I'd like a word with you about your plans for the dig," Toby murmured into Myron's ear.

"Well, say it here—I can't leave." Myron was short.

"In view of everything that has happened, when are you closing it down?"

"Not until I have to." Myron shot him a hard look. "We can't leave, and as long as we have to stay here, we may as well keep at it. I've only got funds for the workmen until the end of the week. After that we'll have to let them go, but we could keep on with the volunteers. As soon as I can, I'm going to wire London to see if they can spare some more money. At least now I've got something to show them for it!" Seeing Toby's disapproving look, his voice rose. "You appear to think this heartless, but to me it seems the only *professional* thing to do. If shutting down activities to mourn, if closing the dig down, would do any *good* to Dr. Pierson, I'd do it. But, situated as we are, this strikes me as the only sensible thing to do: to try to make something out of this mess before we are forced to close down anyway."

"That of course is entirely up to you," Toby said frigidly, realizing he was being unreasonable. "Mrs. Pierson indicated to me she would probably be joining you down here in a day or two."

It was Myron's turn to look shocked. "That's rather unexpected, but if she cares to join us, naturally she will be welcome. We can always use an extra pair of hands, especially experienced ones. What are your plans?"

Toby gazed levelly at him. "I intend to find Dr. Pierson's murderer, and I shall stay here until I do." He was aware that the pair in the trench were listening intently. "I assume you would have no objection to my staying on here while I do this, or of giving assistance if needed."

Myron's eyes dropped. "Naturally," he muttered, "but what sort of assistance?"

"Well, to start with I'd like to see those scroll fragments you've found here, if this is where Bill was working last."

Looking mystified, Myron bent down to the wooden finds tray standing on the edge of the trench and picked up several glassine packets. "The fragments are very small," he remarked as he handed them to Toby, "but one or two have traces of writing, and they'll be a good dating source."

Toby turned his back on the trench on the pretext of seeing the scraps in a better light. As he looked at them, his heart began to pound and his head buzzed uncomfortably. Vellum, he knew, altered in color variably over the years depending on the circumstances of its surroundings. The Jesus document had been a yellowish-gray and remarkably uniform in color. The scrap he had found in the murder cave had been brownish, but this he had assumed could have been caused by its being an outer edge and more exposed, and did not preclude its being from the same scroll. The scraps he was now holding in his hand were a yellowish-gray exactly the same as the Jesus document—so what if Bill had found the scroll right here and not in the cave? His thoughts whirled. If the Jesus scroll had *not* come from the cave, why had Bill been in that particular one? What was so special about it? He would have to go back and look again.

He cleared his throat and said in a very low rumble to Myron, "I have already another favor to ask."

"Yes?"

"You know Dr. Maisler at the Archaeological Museum?"

"Slightly. Why?"

"Well, the very next trip you take to Jerusalem, please take a sufficient sample of these scraps directly to him for C-14 dating. It is extremely important."

"But I can't do that!" Myron protested. "You know full well that all finds are supposed to be kept together until the end of the dig, when an Israeli antiquities inspector has to look them over to decide what goes to them and what we can keep. I could get into all sorts of trouble doing what you ask."

"In this case you are more likely to get into trouble if you don't," Toby rumbled firmly. "I'm afraid I am not at liberty to say why just now, but if you force me I'll have Maisler come down and give you the order himself. He won't like it, because he's an extremely busy man, but I can and will do it." He glared at the younger man, who wilted.

"Then at least tell me why," Goldsmith said.

"I've already told you I'm not free to say. Maisler may choose to enlighten you—that's up to him—but *do* it. Particularly take this scrap, which, if my eyes don't deceive me, has an *iu* on it."

Myron, to cover his angry confusion, gazed closely at the scrap. "Could be anything," he muttered, "but if you are prepared to accept the responsibility . . ."

"I am," Toby barked. "And one last thing—I'd like to take young Dyke with me today into the desert."

"Oh, for God's sake!" Myron's nerves exploded again. "Go ahead, take him and anything else you damn well please, but get off my back! He's not a damn bit of good anyway, the way he's been mooning around since the murder."

He turned his back on Toby and jumped down into the trench with Grayson and Ali. Toby looked at them for a minute or two and at their avidly preoccupied expressions. Suddenly he was sickened by his own occupation and by its narrow single-mindedness. A human being, their colleague, their leader, had been most hideously murdered, but already it was as if he had never existed in their minds as they followed the siren call of the unknown. He felt an urgent need to get away, to breathe the clean air of the desert.

He strode off in search of Robert Dyke, whom he found

gazing unseeingly at a not very interesting section of mud-brick wall a workman was unearthing, supposedly under his direction. "Robert, I need your help again," Toby said as the young man came to with a start. "No horrors this time, I promise you. But I really could use your keen eyes on something. We'll be going into the desert."

"Oh, all right." Robert brightened. "Yes, I'd just as soon get away from here." He gave a little shudder. "It sort of sticks in my gullet, everything going on as usual as if nothing had happened."

Toby clapped a comforting hand on his shoulder. "Me too. Where's Tahir? I'd like a word with him before we go."

"Over in the new cistern, I think." Robert scrambled out of the trench and led the way toward it. Toby saw Carter in deep conversation with Hedecai on another part of the site, and Gregory Vadik was still in the trench with his wife; all present and accounted for, he thought. I hope they'll stay that way until I get back.

He found Tahir at the bottom of the cistern, which was already a good eight feet down, directing the removal of the earth filling by two of the workmen. "I'm back, but I'm going out to the cave again," he called in Turkish. "Anything for me?"

Tahir looked up, his expression surly and preoccupied. "Nothing that will not keep. And I am busy; I cannot go with you."

"Oh no, that's all right." But Toby was a little non-plussed by his cool reception.

"Tahir seems upset," he remarked as they jolted out of camp in the Jeep. "Any idea why?"

"He's been catching it from all quarters," Robert grinned. His spirits were evidently rising with every yard they put between them and the camp. "He got hell from the policeman, then from Myron, and now the Arab workmen are on the point of mutiny because the rumor has gone around that they'll all be laid off at the end of the week. He's pretty fed up about that too, because I think he needs the bread. Did you know he has *three* wives!" His youthful voice was awed. "Just imagine having to keep three of them, and I believe he has about eleven kids as well!"

"Yes, Tahir's a stout Muslim, and the Kurds keep to many of the old ways." Toby chuckled, but then sobered. He had not given much thought to it before, but Tahir was no longer a young man, and such responsibilities, that number of mouths to feed, must weigh heavily on his aging shoulders. He knew Tahir, like his father before him, had no trade but this. And good as he was, excavations tended to be few and far between. How hard pressed for money was he, he wondered uneasily, how desperate? It was not a pretty thought.

This time the journey to the wadi seemed much shorter, and the sun was barely past its zenith when they were once again weaving their way through the dusty vegetation toward the abandoned Jeep. "What are we looking for?" Robert asked.

"I don't know," Toby confessed, "but I am trying to figure out why Dr. Pierson was in that particular cave." They went on past the Jeep until they were standing in the wadi looking directly up into the narrow cleft, which could easily be picked out by the boulder at its entrance. "We have already passed four entrances to caves on that ledge up there, so why that one? Do you see anything special about it?"

Robert craned his neck. "Not a thing," he replied. "Unless you count Lot's wife."

"Lot's wife!" Toby was staggered.

"Yes, you know, that freestanding pillar of rock near Sodom you always see in books on Israel? They call it Lot's wife."

"But I don't understand . . ."

"There, at the very top of the cliff above the cave," Robert pointed out. "See, there's a freestanding pillar just like it, and all the rest of the cliff top up there looks flat. It looks like a giant finger pointing to the sky . . ."

CHAPTER 12

Some time later Toby and Robert were propped up against the boulder outside the murder cave in companionable silence. To make doubly sure he was missing nothing of significance, Toby had checked in every other cave along the ledge up to this one. Outside of some animal droppings in one, he had found nothing. So, he mused to himself, what else was special about this one?

Looking back along the ledge, he realized that the cliff jutted out into a spur here, effectively cutting off the view of the others and of the entrance to the wadi. Hence this cave would be the first one with a direct view to the west. Was this of any significance? He hoisted his binoculars and scanned the barren landscape; nothing. Perhaps the wadi itself. He scanned it slowly, starting from directly underneath and following its twisting course for as far as he could see; a slight anomaly caught his eye.

"See anything?" Robert asked, his voice drowsy with the sun and the peace of the place.

"Um," Toby grunted and handed him the binoculars. "Follow this wadi up from here and tell me if you notice anything."

Robert obediently scanned, then said, a diffident note in his voice, "It's a bit hard to tell with all the shadows now, but it looks as if the vegetation stops further up the wadi there. I can only make out bare rocks further on."

"Yes, a bit odd that. As if this part got water from somewhere and the rest did not. Let's go down and have a closer look."

The ledge they were on gave out a short distance beyond the cave, so they scrambled back the way they had come, which Toby could see was about the only feasible way up the steep cliff face. They hurried up the wadi to where, sure enough, the coarse grass and dusty shrubs suddenly gave out into nothing but rocky scree and bare earth. Toby

111

peered at the cliff face, now deep in shadow, and saw
with quickened interest that there was a difference in it;
for a space of no more than ten feet, the cliff from top to
bottom was cracked and broken, as if some giant hand had
sliced through it and then filled in the gap with rubble of
a darker color than the rest. "It looks to me as if at one
time there was a fissure here, a small gully," he muttered.
"I wonder if it could have been the outlet for a spring."

Robert ran a hand over the lower boulders. "No sign of
water here now. Why do you think that?"

"Apart from the vegetation pattern, look at those lower
boulders—both the color and shape look like water action
to me."

Robert looked up at the dark cliff above. "Might just be
runoff from the top, the fault acting like a funnel when it
rains."

"Possibly, but the boulders down here are very much
darker than the ones above. Damnation! I wish it were not
so shadowy now. We'll have to come back when the sun
is on this face and see more clearly. Then we could follow
the fault back on the cliff top and see where it leads. It
appears to me this filling is the result of some ancient earth-
quake which stopped up a gully and possibly a spring *in*
the gully, from which a certain amount water still gets
through."

"But why is that important? And why a spring anyway?"
Robert's tone was mystified.

Toby could not explain the importance of his hypothetical spring nor of his fragile theory, so he snapped, "Because I'm trying to explain why Dr. Pierson was in *that*
particular cave," which only left the young man more puzzled than ever. "Anyway it is too late to do anything more
about it today," Toby continued testily. "We'd better be
getting back to camp."

"Why couldn't the murderer just have taken Dr. Pierson
to that cave? Maybe it's as simple as that," Robert wondered aloud as he followed him back down the wadi.

Toby shook his head. "No, that won't work. Think about
it. You are holding a man, presumably at gunpoint. You
want to get him out of sight and yet you force him along
a narrow ledge past four other perfectly good caves before
you trap him in the fifth? No, as I see it, the murderer

must have confronted Bill in that cave at the outset, and Bill must have had some reason for being there."

"Well then, how about something in the cave itself?"

"Perhaps, but I don't think so. After all, the cave has been searched with little result." Toby got in the Jeep and started the engine.

Robert climbed in beside him and sighed in frustration. "You know, I have the distinct feeling there's a whole lot more to this than meets the eye—a whole lot you know about and that I haven't been told."

Toby looked at the worried young face with amused approval. "You are a very quick young man, Robert. You happen to be quite right, and for your own good it is going to stay that way. You will just have to trust in me for the moment, but I will say this. We may be on the track to the site of Zadok's tomb." And chuckling grimly to himself, he headed the Jeep back to camp.

He sought out and found Tahir sitting in his own small tent, set a little apart from the big one housing the Arab workmen to mark his senior status. The Kurd was still looking gloomy and preoccupied, so putting aside his own concerns for the moment, Toby asked quietly, "What is the matter, old friend? Can I help in any way?"

The big man sighed. "Things are not good for me; not good at all. When I was to come here, Pierson-*bey* offered me good wages and promised much beyond. I was to stay after the dig ended to finish up and see all well, and for that he promised extra. Now Goldsmith says we are all to go and that he knows nothing of what Pierson-*bey* said. I must leave with the others. I do not know what to do. In June I was to go back to Turkey for Grant-*bey*'s dig on the plateau. My third wife and her children wait for me there in Nigde. I was to stay here until May, but now I cannot stay in Israel if the dig shuts down. I have no money to go back to Kurdistan, no money to send home to my first wife for the many mouths to feed there. I cannot go, I cannot stay. Truly I am an unhappy man."

Toby was in a quandary. Knowing the fierce pride of the Kurds, he realized he could not just offer Tahir money, for that would mortally offend him. He realized besides that this was only part of the problem. With the everlasting touchiness of the political situation in the Middle East, there

was the additional worry of work permits and visas for a
migrant worker such as Tahir. "I'll talk to Goldsmith. I'm
sure something can be worked out," he comforted. "Failing
that, I'm sure Mrs. Pierson will honor the arrangement
Dr. Pierson made with you."

"But where can I go?" Tahir lamented.

"Well, if Grant-*bey* cannot use you earlier than he said,
perhaps you can work for me until then. And if you need
money, I can see to it," Toby soothed.

Tahir looked up with a dangerous flash of his dark eyes.
"I do not seek charity, Glendower-*bey*. I am not a beggar.
You have nothing more to do here, any more than I. I do
not take money I have not earned."

"You forget I have a task here," Toby chided. "I have
still to find Pierson-*bey*'s murderer, and for that I need
help."

The big man continued his own train of thought. "There
has been a curse on this site from the start," he muttered.
"Nothing was as it should be. *I* was to pick the workmen,
I was to be in charge of them, Pierson-*bey* told me; and
then when I come, I find Ali-Muhammed had asked to be
with him and had done all before me."

"Ali volunteered for this? Dr. Pierson didn't send for
him?" Toby said quickly.

"Yes. Pierson-*bey* was surprised but pleased. They had
not met for many years. But it was not right, and something is not right now. Something is going on. If the workmen had been of my choosing, they would not be like this."

"So Ali hired them. Are they Iraqi diggers?" Toby asked,
knowing the traditional hatred between the Kurds and the
Iraqi Arabs.

Tahir shook his head. "No, they are local men. Three
know what they are doing; they have dug before. But
three, I swear, have never so much as wielded a pickax
until now. They are useless. I told Pierson-*bey* this, but
he would do nothing. They whisper among themselves, and
one of them has a gun. That I know."

"Speaking of guns, do you know if anyone else in the
camp besides Dr. Pierson had arms of any kind?"

"The friend of Dr. Pierson, Carter, has one. A gun in
the dashboard compartment of his car. I saw it one day
when he drove me into Jericho. And the big American

has a rifle; he is quite open about it. And in the stores there was some dynamite."

"Dynamite! Whatever for?"

Tahir looked grim. "That is what I would like to know. I found it in the stores hidden among the equipment, and I went to Pierson-*bey* about it. He scoffed at me, would not believe, and when I went to show him it was no longer there."

"Dynamite?" Toby muttered. "What the hell *is* going on here?"

"I do not know, but I do not think it is good."

"Tell me what happened when the news came of Dr. Pierson's death. What was everyone's reaction?"

Tahir grimaced. "The fair-haired policeman came with the constable, and he was furious when he found you were not here. He was so busy shouting at me and threatening that I was hard put to it to keep my eyes about. But they were all shocked, I can tell you that much. Goldsmith went quite green and started to yell at me too for not telling them before. Carter swore and turned on his heel and went stamping off out of camp. Grayson and Ali looked very concerned, but most of all they looked at each other as if the news was bad for them. The girl cried. The Vadiks did not come out of their camper until later. Mrs. Vadik did not seem surprised at the news."

Which amounted to zero, Toby thought. The innocent would be shocked, but then so would the murderer, for it would mean the untimely find of the body had blown apart his scheme to have it appear as a suicide. "Did Officer Baum say anything else?"

"Oh yes, he said a lot. Mostly aimed at the Arabs, but he ranted on about the Bedouin and how when they were captured, it might lead to a clearance of the whole area. I think that also has angered and upset the workmen here."

And, if the murderer was in the camp, it had given him a breathing space to adapt to these new circumstances, Toby reflected. Only in his own mind did the finger of suspicion point toward the expedition. The official view would alter, he was certain, as soon as the results of the autopsy were known, but for now where did it leave him? Nowhere, so far as he could see. For, far from establishing a clearer line to the murderer, so far as motive went, the skein seemed to be more tangled than ever. Were Ali and Grayson involved in some covert terrorist activities, and had Bill stumbled onto this and had to be liquidated? Were the Vadiks involved in it too? Or had someone got wind of the Jesus document, or was it the Zadok treasure scroll they were after?

He shook himself. No, he was not thinking clearly. If Bill had stumbled onto something he shouldn't have, there would be reason to murder but not to torture. Similarly, he did not see how anyone could possibly have known the contents or importance of the Jesus document. Which brought him back to Zadok's treasure and the age-old motive of greed. Bill had been tortured to make him reveal the whereabouts either of the site or of the scroll with the extra information on it. Penny was right; if he could find out what had happened to that, he could see his way clearer. And it also seemed to narrow the field to the hard-pressed Carter and the devious Ali as the most likely candidates. But there were still some unknown factors here. Margaret Cochran had known of it, and Toby had no high opinion of women's discretion. Whom might she not also have told? She had worked with Goldsmith, known about Grayson. Penny would have to find out a lot more about her. In the meantime he would zero in on the Zadok scroll and keep an eye on his two main suspects.

The clanging of an iron pot being beaten lustily brought him out of his reverie. The camp was being summoned to its evening meal. He got up and looked at Tahir, who was gazing at him in somber silence. "Try not to worry," he comforted. "We'll find a solution to your problems. We will talk later." And Toby made his way to the mess tent.

The table had been rearranged and appeared to him a lot more crowded, as his eyes adjusted from the dim light outside to the harsh glare within. Bill's place at the head of the table had now been taken by Goldsmith, who was flanked by Grayson on his right and Vadik on his left. Carter occupied Myron's former seat at the foot of the table, and the only space left was between him and Vashti Vadik, who sat on the left of her husband and opposite Ali. She glanced up at him with the same faintly frightened, pinched look as he took his place beside her with a muttered apology. He helped himself to some white goat cheese and bread as a steaming plate of the inevitable lamb stew was put before him, saw that Carter was deep in low-voiced conversation with Hedecai, so turned his attention back to Vashti, who was pushing the stew around on her plate and not eating.

"The camp cook seems to have a very limited repertoire," he remarked, trying to put her at ease.

She gave him a quick look. "Oh, this is very good," she whispered. "It's just that I have no appetite." She shivered suddenly. "You do not feel it?"

"Feel what?"

"The hostile vibrations. They are all around us. There is evil here; I wish we had not come." There was a note of anguish in the low voice.

"Why did you then?" he probed gently.

"Because Gregor wished it. My gift, he says, must be used, even if it is a painful one."

"I must confess I know little of these things," Toby rumbled, he hoped soothingly, "but I would be most interested to learn more about it. How do your—er—messages come?"

"Oh, many, many ways." She nervously rolled a scrap of bread into a pellet and chased it around on the table with a small, pointed finger. "Sometimes it is a voice, sometimes a scene, sometimes just a name, and with it comes a feeling."

"And in this case?"

"The name Wadi Mugharid, a man in pain, a bearded man and a great finger pointing to the sky."

Robert, across the table from Toby, had been sitting in silence and listening. He leaned forward excitedly and opened his mouth to speak. Toby glared at him and shook his head warningly, so he subsided. "And?" Toby prompted.

"And a feeling of being lost and in danger."

"But how did you come up with Dr. Pierson from all that?"

She started to look frightened again. "I don't know. I mean I didn't; Gregor did. He has powers too, but not as mine."

Toby looked at the big man beside her, whose bass voice was dominating his end of the table. Whatever powers Gregory Vadik had, he was sure they were very much of this world and not of the world beyond. Nevertheless he was impressed in spite of himself by the convincing tone of the frail woman beside him. Either she was a genuine telepath or she was a great actress and knew about the site of the cave already.

Her next words shook him. "Tell me," she whispered, "where was Dr. Pierson found? The policeman did not say, save that it was in the wilderness."

"In a cave whose entrance had been blocked off." He did not elaborate.

She shook her head perplexedly. "I do not understand the finger then. It seemed to have great meaning, for even in his pain he thought of it. Do *you* know?"

Toby squelched Robert with another glare. "I'm afraid not." She sighed and fell silent, staring unseeingly at Ali across from her.

He became aware of Carter's gaze on him. "What was all that about?" the fair Englishman asked.

Toby shrugged. "It's beyond me."

"Did you see Valerie?" John Carter asked in a suitably hushed voice. "How is the poor girl taking it?"

"Oh, very well, considering"—Toby tried not to sound sarcastic—"though naturally it was a great shock."

"I must go up to Jerusalem and see what I can do before she goes home, poor girl. A devilish thing to have to face, devilish!"

"She isn't planning to go home," Toby murmured mildly. "In fact she may be coming down here in the next day or two to help with the dig."

Toby could have sworn that the shock and discomfiture in John Carter's face was the real thing as he stuttered, "She's coming here?"

"So she said; in fact she seemed quite set on it."

There was a sudden urgent tugging on his jacket and he turned to face Vashti, whose green eyes were wide and fixed. "This woman you speak of—she is fair, very fair?"

"Mrs. Pierson? Yes, she is a blonde."

"Mrs. Pierson! Oh no!" Her hands fluttered to her mouth. "She must not come here. She *must* not!"

"Why?"

The eyes looked through and beyond him. "She brings danger, terrible danger. No, you must stop her!"

"Mrs. Pierson is in danger?"

"There is danger all around her; to her, to you, to us all." She gave a little gasp and slumped in her seat.

Her husband belatedly became aware that something was wrong. "What is it, Vashti?" He put a beefy arm around the half-fainting woman and glared at Toby. "What have you said to her?"

"No, Gregor, it is not his fault." She put a pleading hand to his face. "Take me back to the camper, please?"

He stood up and effortlessly gathered the frail figure into his arms, murmuring in a tongue that was strange to Toby's ear.

The rest of the table fell into a startled silence, but this too was broken by a further interruption. Suddenly the tent flap was thrown back. Officer Baum, his springy, fair hair glinting like a golden crown, stepped into the light. He had a triumphant expression on his face as he rattled off a long speech directed at Myron Goldsmith, whose face broke into a delighted grin.

"Please translate," Toby boomed impatiently in German.

The smile froze on Baum's face and he shot a furious glance at him. "I have just said that no one has any further need to worry," he snapped. "The murderers of Dr. Pierson have been captured red-handed and are under lock and key in Engedi. In a day or two you will all be free to go."

CHAPTER 13

"I don't believe one damn word of it," Toby fumed into the phone. "I think that young fool Baum is so pig-headed that he is prepared to railroad the first Bedouin he has laid hands on. What does Abrams think, and what about the autopsy?"

"Well, although he is the first policeman I can recall who didn't hate me on sight, I'm not exactly in his confidence," Penny confessed at her end of the line. "He's being very cautious because, according to this Officer Baum, one of the Arabs has already confessed. I gathered Abrams did not think too much of that, since Baum is not noted for his gentle ways, but he just doesn't have all the facts as yet nor is the autopsy available—or, at least, not to me. I've phoned him twice today about it."

"Then, damn it, go camp on his doorstep," Toby snarled. "It's extremely important that I know."

"It's no use getting snappish with me," Penny bristled. "I've worries of my own and I can't be in two places at once. I have been haunting the British School hoping Margaret Cochran will show up. They are still being obstinate about giving me her address, and the news of the murder was on the local radio and TV this morning, so I'm worried about her."

"Get it from Abrams then! They must know where all the foreigners live, particularly if they work here."

"Oh, I never thought of that." Penny mentally kicked herself.

"And when you do find her," Toby persisted, "try to find out anything else about the scroll scrap she gave to Bill. Whether she ever read it, or if there is a translation, or what. That's very important, too, because I think I may be onto something. And another thing—whatever you do, don't let Valerie come down here at the moment."

"How the devil am I supposed to do that?" Penny complained. "Since firing me, the grieving widow has hardly deigned to drop a word in my direction. She spends most of the time on the telephone or talking to reporters. Anyway, why shouldn't she come down? It might shake things loose."

"Because I think it would be dangerous just now." Toby could not explain why he had been so impressed, in spite of himself, by Vashti Vadik. Her strange utterances, whether fake or real, had struck a chord in him and he believed in the danger. "Just try and put her off for a day or two at least, until I can see my own way clearer down here."

"It would certainly help if you would give me some valid reason as to why she shouldn't." Penny was impatient. "You are not telling me everything, Toby, and that's not fair."

"It's nothing concrete," he fussed, "but Vashti Vadik was very upset at the thought of her coming, and I must say I think there may be something in her damned powers. She said some remarkable things yesterday."

"That's about the last thing I ever expected to hear from you!" Penny sounded highly amused. "I hope I get to meet this fabulous person, but in the meantime I'll see what I can do about Valerie. No promises, though. Can you call me back tonight? I'll go and have another nag about the autopsy."

"And while you're at it get in touch with Maisler too," Toby added, and told her of the new fragments that he hoped would be in Maisler's hands before the day was out. "I'm almost certain they are from the Jesus scroll. In which case the scrap I found in the cave is out of the running—another reason I desperately need more information on the Zadok scroll. Do you have anything else for me? Any news from Edwards or that old student of yours?"

"I've been so busy chasing after Abrams and Margaret Cochran that I haven't had a moment to contact Angela," Penny said in an aggrieved tone, "and I'd better hurry up or she'll be off with her husband on a VIP tour."

"Oh," Toby said indifferently, not realizing he had just been given a vital bit of information. "Well, I'll call you back about six tonight. Hope you have something for me then." He rang off and walked out of the small restaurant from which he had phoned, and looked gloomily around at the small, bustling town of Jericho. It had changed out of all recognition from the sleepy village he remembered twenty-five years ago. There were sparkling new blocks of ultramodern apartments, and the town was now ringed with flourishing little kibbutzim spreading the leafy green fruit plantations of this constant oasis in growing tentacles into the heart of the desert. He walked along the busy main street lined with red-flowering poinciana trees, unaccountably depressed by the exuberance of all the life around him. His steps led him to the center of town, where the Spring of Elisha still gushed forth its life-giving waters, which for the past nine thousand years had drawn men to this most ancient of towns.

Opposite the spring loomed the seventy-foot mound of Tell el Sultan, the remains of the ancient cities of Jericho, its face scarred and pockmarked by many excavations. For old times' sake he decided on a stroll to the top, hoping to lighten his mood by a remembrance of things past. His path took him by the deep cutting which had in its depths the first ancient wall and stone tower that the Neolithic people of Jericho had built to keep invaders away from their never-failing spring. He stopped at the top of the flight of steep steps leading down into it, debating whether to enter the cool depths, and absentmindedly noted that there were some tourists already clustered around the base of the old stone tower. He was about to move on, shrinking from the companionship of his fellow men, when something familiar clicked in his mind, his vision cleared and he zeroed in on the small group below him.

He drew in his breath sharply as he realized what he was seeing. Gregory Vadik had his back toward the stone tower, and behind his bulky frame Toby could just make out the small figure of Vashti. Around Gregory were circled three men, two in ordinary street clothes, the third with the head gear, if not the clothes, of the desert Arab. Toby was too far away to hear what they were saying, but from their strained, taut figures and gestures, it was evident that they were angry and threatening. Even as he watched, the hand of the desert Arab went to his waist and reappeared holding a knife.

Toby decided to abandon his role of disinterested spectator and take a hand. "Hello, down there!" he called out. "I wondered where you had got to. Hadn't we better be going?"

The group froze, and the knife disappeared as quickly as it had appeared. Gregory Vadik looked up, sudden hope in his face. "Ah, there you are, Professor," he boomed back. "Yes, be right with you. Are the others ready?"

"Yes, they are waiting for us," Toby roared, taking his cue.

The men stood their ground for a moment, while Gregory, never taking his eyes off them for an instant, stepped sideways, put his arm around his wife's shoulders and, with a sudden rush, shouldered his way through them, pushing her ahead of him up the narrow steps. Three dark, angry faces turned up to Toby, then the little group below dissolved and melted away into the shadows of the deep pit. Vashti and Gregory reached the top of the steps panting slightly; she was pale, and there were beads of perspiration on Gregory's brow.

"Trouble?" inquired Toby with a hint of irony.

The big man recovered fast. "No. Thanks to you," he replied. "Very grateful to you, Professor. Just some of these fake antique touts trying to make a quick sale. They sometimes turn nasty if they have you outnumbered."

"Oh really?" Toby murmured, never taking his eyes off Vashti's face, whose eloquent expression gave the lie to her husband's glib answer. "Then I suppose I had better abandon my plans for a wander through the ruins."

"If you know what is good for you." There was a grim note in Gregory Vadik's deep voice. "Israel can still be a dangerous place. But come, let me buy you a drink. I know an excellent al fresco bar near here. A beautiful day, is it not?"

"Thank you, but no," Toby rumbled. "I really must be getting back to Wadi Mugharid. Are you going there?"

"No, we've some supplies still to get," Gregory said easily, "but perhaps you will join us some other time."

Toby went to move off, but Vashti put a small hand on his arm and looked up at him, an appeal in her green eyes. "You are a good man, I think—a very good man," she whispered. "Be careful, Sir Tobias, please be careful! Go to Jerusalem, do not stay at Wadi Mugharid." And turning, she fled down the narrow pathway.

Gregory looked after her, shrugged and smiled. "My wife has taken quite a fancy to you, it seems, Professor, but she is very temperamental. Do not alarm yourself at her fancies."

"Oh, I won't," Toby murmured. "And the feeling is mutual, so I have some advice for you, Mr. Vadik. Whatever you are up to in this country, I advise you to abandon it and move on, for your wife's sake. No good will come of it."

The big man all but laughed in his face. "So nice of you to care," he said sarcastically and set off after his wife.

"But what the hell *are* you up to?" Toby muttered despondently as he gazed after them, and his depression returned in full force.

When Penny put down the phone at her end she dithered around the small hotel lobby like a bemused mouse. What to do? She hated to beard Inspector Abrams again, fearing to wear out her welcome, and yet she was increasingly concerned about Margaret Cochran, who somewhere in this electric, crowded city was alone with her grief. A bright idea came to her. "The Department of Antiquities! *They* ought to know because of the work permit, and at least they are helpful."

They were and did, and cursing herself for not thinking of them before, Penny hurried toward the Old City, the vital address and a map clutched tightly in her hand. She entered its narrow confines through the Jaffa Gate and bustled her way through the pressing throngs of pilgrims, tourists, street sellers and a few native inhabitants jostling one another in the narrow cobbled streets. The crowd in the Via Dolorosa was almost suffocating in its density, but she finally located the right narrow street opening off it which heralded her goal. "If she's after atmosphere, she's certainly got it in spades!" she muttered, peering dubiously into the dark cavern of a small gateway which bore the right number. She passed into a little courtyard and came face to face with a black-veiled woman, who took one look at her and pointed a startled finger to an upper balcony. "Thanks, friend, good thinking!" Penny congratulated, and hurried up the rickety wooden stairway to a solid-looking door at the top. There was a handwritten card tacked on it with "Margaret Cochran" and the British School of Jerusalem address written on it.

"Pay dirt," Penny exulted and pounded on the door. There was dead silence so she pounded again. This time there was a shuffling on the other side and a weak "Who is it?"

"It's Penny Spring, Miss Cochran," Penny called out, "I've been worried about you. Please let me in. This is no time for you to be alone. Please let me help you!"

The door slowly swung wide and Margaret Cochran blinked blearily at her. Penny was appalled. It was as if the attractive, vibrant shell of the woman had imploded and cracked, leaving her stooped and shriveled. The long, fair hair hung down in tangled disarray, the full figure was flabby and drooping, the face swollen by tears into a grotesque mask, and Penny could smell the sour reek of liquor on her breath. "Oh God, oh dear God!" said Margaret Cochran, and big tears welled out of the bloodshot blue eyes, spilling down the flabby cheeks as she gathered a thin housecoat about her and turned away.

Penny marched in behind her and firmly closed the door. "I've been looking for you ever since I heard the terrible news," she stated flatly. "When did you eat last? The first thing I'm going to do is get some food into you. Then we can talk."

Margaret slumped down on a small couch that had evidently been serving her as a bed as well. Beside it was a brass-tray table laden with a collection of empty vodka bottles and some dirty glasses. She shook her head dazedly. "I don't know. I don't care," she sobbed. "I've been trying to get up enough nerve to end it all. Oh, *why* did it have to happen!"

"Killing yourself will solve precisely nothing. I'm surprised at you. Here we are with a fight on our hands and you let yourself go like this!" Penny snapped, and made for the tiny kitchen she glimpsed beyond. "First of all I'll make us some good strong tea." She proceeded to brew the tea, make an omelette, slice up some tomatoes and toast some very stale bread, load up a tray with the results and stagger back in with it to the accompaniment of the hopeless sobbing of her patient. She managed to get the food and drink down the bemused woman, alternately scolding and coaxing, until a little color appeared in Margaret's ashen-gray cheeks. When Penny was certain that what she had got down her was likely to stay down, she topped off her efforts with a couple of aspirin from the bottle she always carried in her tote bag and sat back to survey her handiwork.

Margaret sat up straighter and let out a quivering sigh. "Now I know what hell is like," she said simply. "What *am* I to do?"

"I know you've had a great shock and a great loss, and it is natural to grieve," Penny returned, "but to give up like this I'm sure is the last thing Bill would want you to do. That he died tragically trying to build the future you and he planned is a terrible thing, but it will be a double tragedy if you let yourself be destroyed, too. His murderer must be found, and you can help us find him. You owe Bill that much."

Margaret looked blankly at her. "But the radio said an arrest had been made," she faltered.

"I know, but that's nonsense." Penny was firm. "They've got the wrong men. It looks as if Bill was killed because someone was onto the fact he was after the treasure. Toby thinks someone at the camp *now*, someone who may have killed him for that scroll scrap with the treasure information on it. That's where you come in. I didn't press you on this before, but I must now. You have seen the scroll. Bill must have made a translation. Do you know what it said? Do you have a copy? It really is vital that you tell us everything you know."

"But if that comes out, Bill's reputation will be ruined," Margaret stammered. "I can't, I won't do that. It's all he had left."

"It won't come out. There are so many other things involved now that Toby can cover up, and you know he will, but he *must* have the information. I can't tell you what other things are involved; some I don't know myself, others Toby has to keep quiet for the moment, but you know we were friends of Bill's, so you can and must trust our discretion."

Margaret put a hand to her forehead. "I'm so mixed up, my head is so muzzy, I don't know that I can be of much help. I did see Bill's translation when he first made it, but that was so long ago. I'm not sure I can recall anything meaningful."

"You simply must try. Any little detail might help. Just begin, for instance, with the translation. Did he make copies? Did he stash any of them somewhere for safekeeping? If so, where? Think!"

The bedraggled woman moaned softly. "I think I need a drink."

"By the looks of all this, you've done a sight too much of that already," Penny said severely.

Margaret gave her a haunted look. "I can't help it. I need it. Particularly now. Just one, I promise."

"Oh, all right!" Penny snapped. "Do you have any more?"

"There should be another bottle under the sink."

The drink was found, poured and tossed back in a strained silence. Margaret put down the glass and gave a relieved sigh. "Ah, that's better! I can think now. Bill had two translations. One he kept with him when I came out here, one he gave me with the scroll. The other must be still among his papers in England, because he took both of mine, as I told you before."

So Valerie might have seen it, might know also, Penny thought, but said nothing. Instead she took a copy of the Allegro translation of the Copper Scroll out of her bag and handed it to Margaret. "Here, this might help. This after all is the main source for the whole idea. Can you recall what *additional* details were on the scroll fragment?"

Margaret studied it, her brow wrinkled with effort. "It was something to do with the entranceway to the Garden of Zadok, and there was some reference to the Essene community at Mugharid. I remember Bill saying it must be almost a hidden site with a narrow entranceway, and the scrap had directions to find that entrance. There was something about a spring in the Valley of Zadok. And something else about the shadow of the Finger of God pointing the way to the spring. This was what puzzled Bill the most, that and an obscure passage about time. It seemed to refer to a time of year and a time of day, but he couldn't seem to pin it down. I know he began to think that the Finger of God was probably a marker of some kind."

"Did he say anything to you about having found it?"

Margaret shook her head. "No, unless that vague reference he made the last time he called meant that, but it did not sound like it. And that is *all* I know."

Penny started to make notes, hoping that they would make some kind of sense to Toby because they certainly didn't make any to her. Aware that she was treading now on very delicate ground, she asked, "And what were your ongoing plans? I mean, what did you plan to do when Bill located the treasure?"

Tears once more brimmed in Margaret's eyes. "I told you," she whispered, "we were going to get the money and go away together."

"Yes, but how? If the treasure was as stated, its principal worth would have been in the book containing clues to the other treasure locations. Bill couldn't sell the book on the open market. How was he planning to get the money for it? He would have had to find a buyer."

A faint gleam came into the faded woman's eyes. "Oh yes, he said that was all taken care of. When the time came, he said, he had a buyer who would come and pay him what he asked."

"But who?" Penny almost shouted.

"I don't know. Just someone who would be there when the time came." A look of terror came into her face.

Penny nodded at her grimly. "I see you have just thought of it too. Someone *else*, then, must have known what Bill was after. Someone besides you and Valerie and possibly Carter. Tell me, does the name Vadik mean anything to you?" But she found she was talking to empty air; Margaret Cochran had fainted dead away.

CHAPTER 14

Penny was in a dour mood as she made her way out of the old city, through the Damascus Gate this time, and started the long hike back to her hotel through the modern bustle of the Nablus Road. She had got nothing further out of Margaret Cochran, who on coming out of her faint had collapsed into hopeless sobbing once more. Penny, feeling she had had all she could stand, had managed to get a couple of sleeping tablets into her, confiscated the rest, tucked her into her bed and taken her leave, promising to return in the evening.

She did not know whether to believe Margaret's assertion that the name Vadik meant nothing to her, but the woman was in such a shaky state that she had no heart for further browbeating. She felt in need of a little rest and a long think, but she was destined not to realize either. No sooner was she inside the hotel than the manager pounced on her to announce that there had been a message from police headquarters and would she go there at once. "Oh, dear God, what now!" Penny said crossly and bustled out again.

She was somewhat soothed when, instead of being kept waiting as usual, she was ushered immediately into Inspector Abrams's office and settled with a weary sigh of relief into his visitor's chair. The suave inspector looked with some inner amusement at the small, crumpled-looking woman, her mousy hair standing on end, her attractively ugly face shining with her exertions, but he did not underestimate the intelligence that shone from the shrewd hazel eyes. Ability, he thought to himself, sometimes showed up in the most odd packaging, and it did not surprise him that the equally bizarre and formidable Tobias Glendower had chosen this particular woman as his confidante.

"Good of you to come so quickly, Dr. Spring. Knowing Sir Tobias is anxious for news, I thought you would want to know the results of the autopsy as soon as possible."

Penny eagerly took the sheaf of papers he handed her, saying, "I can keep these?"

He hesitated. "No, I'm afraid not. You must realize this is highly unofficial. Knowing Sir Tobias's concern for his friend, I felt his request not unreasonable, so I do not mind his having the information, but the papers must stay here."

Her face fell. "May I make notes then?"

Again he hesitated. "Yes, providing only you and Sir Tobias have access to them."

She nodded and dived into her large handbag, reappearing with sundry scraps of paper and a pen. Then, knitting her brows, she began to study the papers and scribble furiously.

The shrilling telephone claimed Abrams, but as he answered it, he continued to watch her, for her absorbed concentration impressed him. Something in the report appeared to puzzle her and she held up the sheet she had been writing on as if to study it more closely. He read what was on the back and his eyebrows rose a fraction. The routine matter settled, he cradled the phone and said, "If there are any technicalities I can clarify for you, I shall be happy to do so."

"Oh thank you, yes, well I think I get the gist of it," she muttered absently. "Maybe if I put it in my own words and feed it back to you, you can tell me if I'm wrong."

"Whenever you are ready."

"The cause of death was the second bullet, which grazed the heart, the first bullet in the throat being a missed shot or to stop him talking. Both bullets came from his own gun. He had been bound with a nylon rope, and the burns were inflicted by either a cigarette or a thin cheroot. The time of death would have been approximately thirty-eight hours before Toby discovered the body, in other words sometime on the day we arrived in Israel?"

"Right so far," he encouraged. "With the lapse of time between death and the finding of the body, it is difficult to pin down the exact hour of death."

"There had been a severe blow on the back of the head

and laceration of the scalp some time previous to death. I suppose that's when the murderer knocked him out in the first place," she went on.

"That, of course, is only a supposition, but a likely one. Dr. Pierson was a fairly powerful man, so unless several people were involved, it is unlikely that he could have been subdued without other traces of a fight. There were no bruised knuckles or other bruises of that nature, so it is a fair assumption that he was taken unaware and struck down from behind."

Penny considered this and did not much care for the implications. It indicated either a superquiet murderer who could have crept up on Bill in the cave without giving himself away, or someone he trusted and did not suspect! And that certainly would seem to rule out either Grayson or Carter, two of Toby's prime suspects. "There's a bit here I do not understand," she said slowly. "The burns on the genital area were not made by the same means as the others. Traces of some substance were found, but I do not recognize the term used."

"May I see?" Abrams said smoothly and turned her notes toward him. "Ah, yes, it's the chemical notation for butane gas, Dr. Spring. Traces of a type of butane were found all around the genital area."

"You mean the sort they use in racing cars—what is it, superethyl?"

"No, the sort of gas they put in many cigarette lighters these days." His tone was noncommittal.

"So *that* rules out the Bedouin who have been arrested," Penny said with prompt relief.

"Does it? Why do you say that?"

"A Bedouin with a butane lighter! Whoever heard of such a thing!" she exclaimed.

"Oh, the modern Bedouin are a far cry from those of the days of Lawrence," Abrams said dryly. "Transistor radios blare from the black tents nowadays. They take their time from digital watches, not the sun, and they are as free to buy a butane lighter from any tobacconist or bar in Israel as I am."

"But it's not *likely*," she protested. "Most Bedouin are still strict Muslims who neither smoke nor drink. And don't tell me they use such things to light their campfires, because you probably know as well as I do that a lighter is the worst thing to use to get a fire started."

Abrams changed direction. "For all we know, it could have belonged to Dr. Pierson himself."

"He was a nonsmoker," Penny said quickly.

"You know that for a fact?"

"Yes, I'm almost certain of it." She nearly added that he would not have dared, knowing Valerie's aversion, but thought better of it. "Anyway, what about the other things—the heel mark in the cave and the ashes. Surely those point away from them?"

"There are still some things to be clarified," Abrams agreed.

"Well, what about the ashes? Can't you identify the tobacco? That would certainly clarify matters."

A hint of a smile appeared on his firm mouth. "Contrary to your, er, famous detective, Sherlock Holmes, it is an extremely difficult matter to identify tobacco ash, particularly when it is so mixed in with dirt, as this was. We are running further tests, but I very much doubt whether we'll get much more than we already have."

"I must say I agree with Sir Tobias," she said stoutly. "Everything about the murder appears to me to be a one-man operation, and a man with a very different cultural orientation than those poor Bedouin. Have you questioned them? Are *you* satisfied with this 'confession'?"

Abrams's face hardened. "No. They have been brought to Jerusalem, but I have not as yet questioned them. The man who confessed has been taken to the hospital." A spasm of anger constricted the muscles of his jaw. "It is a fact that he was in possession of Dr. Pierson's watch. It is a fact that Dr. Pierson was robbed. It is also, unfortunately, a fact that the officer from Engedi is well known for his dislike of the Bedouin, so no, I am not completely satisfied."

Under the pretext of arranging her notes in order, he shuffled through the papers before him until he came to the sheet he sought. Turning it over, he read what it contained and then said in a grim, even tone, "You are interested in the Dead Sea Scrolls, Dr. Spring?"

Damnation! Penny thought, as she realized belatedly she had used the back of the Copper Scroll notes for her own. Why the devil don't I keep a neat little black note-book like Toby? But it was too late for that. "Er, yes," she said lamely, "I understand the Wadi Mugharid dig is on another Essene monastery so I was, er, boning up."

Abrams's fist came crashing down on the desk, causing her to jump. "That won't do, Dr. Spring!" he thundered. "I am not a fool. I should like to know exactly *why* Sir Tobias is so certain someone in that camp is responsible for this murder, as he has been from the first. What is going on down there? I may point out that it is an extremely serious matter to conceal evidence from the police, no matter how high-minded the motives. I want to know what is behind this and what, despite my warnings to stay clear of it, Sir Tobias is up to."

Oh dear, that's torn it! Penny thought in dismay, but she tried to put on a brave and, she hoped, an innocent front. "Believe me, Sir Tobias has given you the evidence he found, and neither of us would dream of *obstructing* the police. You must see that from our records. And, as he has told you, there are people at the camp whose presence he cannot explain, and that disturbs him."

"No, I'm afraid that won't do." Abrams favored her with a long, hard stare. "Why *this* particular extract from the Copper Scroll?"

Wishing fervently that he were not so well informed, Penny decided to get herself off the hook and Valerie on. "I really don't know. When Mrs. Pierson first called on Sir Tobias, worried about her husband's unaccountable absence, she brought that with her. I was not present. You will have to ask her or Sir Tobias. I just cannot tell you."

"But you have made additional notes on this," he continued mercilessly.

"Oh, I just jotted down some extra things Sir Tobias mentioned." She was studiedly vague.

"And what was the source of his information?"

"I've no idea. You'll have to ask him," she fired back, hoping wildly she could contact Toby before the inspector did. "And speaking of Sir Tobias, he particularly asked me if you could give him any additional information on the Vadiks."

Abrams refused to be sidetracked. "Dr. Spring, William

Pierson was *tortured* and murdered. That is about the only thing that is predisposing me at the moment to think that the Bedouin were not involved, because, while it is entirely possible that they may have shot a man in the commission of a robbery, it is not like them to resort to torture *unless there was a strong motive."*

"Just what I've been saying!" Penny broke in, but he ignored her.

"It never entered my mind before," he went on, tapping the paper with a heavy finger, "but if Dr. Pierson had stumbled on something in connection with this lost site, that *would* be a motive, and if Sir Tobias is covertly following this trail for reasons of his own, he may be in equally great danger."

Penny thought frantically. What harm could it do Bill now if his hunt for the treasure came out? Not too much, so far as she could see, but she was too pressed and too confused to think out all the angles, so she decided to stonewall until she had time to talk it over with Toby. "As you say, it would be a motive," she agreed, "but again, you would have to ask Sir Tobias. I am only a messenger in all this."

Like hell you are, Abrams thought, looking at the resolute little face. He sighed in exasperation. "I can only repeat to you what I have already told him. These are dangerous matters he has got himself involved in, and he should get out and leave it to the police. You ask me about the Vadiks, and I can only say that Gregory Vadik is a dangerous man. He has been arrested in nearly every Near Eastern country, including this one, and he has always gone free. He has friends in very high places, and the true nature of his work remains a mystery—at least to me. Some say he is a double agent for the Americans and Russians and so valuable to both that he is untouchable. Others say his power comes from the big-money interests behind him. Whatever the source of it, his appearance anywhere always signals trouble for someone. I am aware, since I have made inquiries, that you and Sir Tobias have been involved in two previous murder cases that were brought to successful conclusions, but I may point out that you were amateurs going up against amateurish criminals. If Vadik is involved in this, he is a *professional,* and one of the best; Sir Tobias would not stand a chance against him. I have a very good mind to Have Sir Tobias brought to Jerusalem in protective custody in order to head off further trouble."

"Please don't do that," Penny said quickly. "At least give me the chance to talk to him first. Believe me, if he is onto something, I can persuade him to tell me about it. I know him, and if you do bring him to Jerusalem, you'll just bring out his stubborn streak and you won't get anywhere. I am the last person who would want to see him in danger."

Abrams looked searchingly at her. "Yes, I can believe that. But if I do not hear from you in the next twenty-four hours, I shall have to act. It will be for Sir Tobias's best interests, I assure you. In the meantime I shall get to the bottom of this Bedouin business." He gave a dismissive nod, and a much-shattered Penny made her way out.

Twenty-four hours! What should she do? She made for the nearest restaurant and absentmindedly ordered herself a substantial lunch. As she thought about it, she realized Toby would never admit anything about the hunt for Zadok's treasure until the Jesus document had been authenticated and Bill's claim to posthumous immortality put beyond question. "Oh dear!" she mourned. "How on earth can I bring that about? Get after Maisler, get after Edwards, but then what?" She found herself looking at a neat ring of empty plates and with a distinct case of heartburn. "No time like the present, I suppose," she groaned and went off in search of Maisler.

After the usual hassle to get in, she finally was face to face with the gnomelike archaeologist and took an immediate fancy to him; Einstein had always been one of her favorite characters. He did not appear overjoyed to see her, but when she explained her errand and passed on Toby's message about the new scroll scraps from the site, he became at least interested. "It is *terribly* important we get the dates on them as quickly as possible," she pleaded. "Are any of the results in yet?"

Maisler shrugged. "These things take time. I do have a preliminary report on the scrap Glendower found in the murder cave. It dates from the second half of the first century A.D.; if it is part of the same scroll, then the Jesus document is a fake."

"Oh, good!" Penny exclaimed to his amazement. "That's one less worry. Oh, didn't I mention that Professor Glendower now thinks the Jesus document came from the site? And these new scraps I mentioned are part of the same scroll?"

"No, you didn't," he said with exasperated interest; she was beginning to amuse him. "But do go on."

On she went and before long was pouring a cautious portion of her troubles into his not unwilling ear. "Couldn't you call the police," she coaxed, "and tell them about the scrap and say he has to stay down there for the moment because you are expecting new developments? I mean it's such a pity if he has to be dragged away just when things are getting so interesting at the excavation."

"I'll have to think about it." Maisler was becoming intrigued. "But I really don't want to do anything before the fate of the Jesus document is decided. With a find of this importance you must see how vital is that no premature news leaks out. If it is a forgery it would be most embarrassing to us all."

"May I call you about it later today then?" she urged.

"Well, I'll try and hurry them up; but I can promise nothing," he agreed, and with that she had to be satisfied.

Feeling more than a little worn with all this deception, she got a cab back to the hotel, still pondering how to save Toby from Abrams's well-meant intentions. Her hopes rose slightly when she found a message in her pigeonhole at the desk asking her to call Garth Edwards as soon as possible.

She got through at once and an excited Garth bubbled into the phone, "It's come! And it's great news! Just heard over the transatlantic phone. The scrap we took of the Jesus document dates into the first quarter of the first century A.D. It's genuine! But the other thing—that bit Glendower found in the cave—is not the same. Second half of the first century A.D., so that's not where it came from. But how's that for American efficiency!"

"God bless America!" Penny said with fervor. "Now I can give Toby some of the breathing room he needs."

CHAPTER 15

It was too late, after his strange encounter with the Vadiks and with his telephone date with Penny set for early evening, for Toby to get back to the desert. Although he was itching to test out his theory by further exploration, he realized it would have to wait for at least another day and, for want of any better ideas, decided to head back to the site to see if the scriptorium had yielded any new excitement.

In the gully below the camp, he stopped his Jeep and walked the short distance to where Carter had indicated he kept his car. It turned out to be a white Mercedes sports coupe, an expensive toy just as Toby had anticipated, but now much begrimed with desert dust. He tentatively tried the doors, hoping to get a look at the gun Tahir had spotted in the glove compartment, but they were locked. One feature about the car struck him as being a bit unusual: Carter had had it fitted with the special balloon tires which make desert traveling a lot easier, but which for the short season of the Wadi Mugharid dig seemed to Toby a rather unnecessary expense. That is, unless Carter was planning on more extensive desert travel for reasons of his own. Something else he would have to check on.

A glance at his watch showed him the camp lunch and rest break should just about be over, so he climbed back into his own humbler transport and jolted on up to the plateau. He decided to have a word with Carter, hoping to enlist his aid in keeping Valerie away from the site. Judging by Carter's reactions to her impending arrival, Toby felt this was something on which he could count.

The camp was sunk in somnolent quiet, and he saw that all the vehicles were gone. Vadik's camper had not returned, Grayson's Land Rover was missing, as was the other Jeep. Toby hoped this meant Goldsmith had taken his exhortations to heart and was on the way to Maisler with the new scroll scraps. It looked to him as if everyone was already back at work on the site, but he decided to check Carter's tent anyway. If he was there, all to the good; if he wasn't, he would have a quiet snoop through his things.

He was almost up to the tent when a figure ran out, startling him. It was one of the Arab basket boys, a slim, effeminate-looking youth of about seventeen who was clutching a couple of Israeli pound notes in his hand.

"What were you doing in there?" Toby thundered in his surprise.

The youth gave him a sweeping upward glance of his large, long-lashed dark eyes, giggled shrilly and, before Toby could lay a hand on him, scuttled off in the direction of the site.

"Carter!" Toby called. He plunged into the tent and stopped in shock as he saw Carter sprawled naked on the camp cot, his jowly face puffy with sated passion.

Looking up into Toby's startled face, he gave a feeble laugh and pulled his trousers over himself. "Have a heart, old chap! Not very discreet bursting in on a fellow Britisher like this. Didn't they teach you the art of discretion at Winchester? You wouldn't have lasted long at my public school." Though shaken, he was by far the more collected of the two.

"I do apologize," Toby stuttered out, "but when I saw the boy coming out, I naturally thought he'd been pilfering, so I . . ."

"Well, now you know different." Carter's voice had taken a disagreeable edge. "Do you mind waiting outside? I'll be with you shortly."

"Er, of course!" Toby stumbled out again and stood blinking in agitation at the blazing disc of the sun. In some things he was extremely prudish, and this happened to be one of them, so his sense of outrage added to the chaos of his thoughts. This was the last thing he had expected! No wonder, if all Penny's information on Valerie was correct, Carter was so upset at the idea of her coming to the site! Toby was no expert on these matters, but he vaguely supposed Carter was bisexual. His cogitations were interrupted by John Carter emerging from the tent patting

his thinning fair hair carefully into place. He had completely recovered his sangfroid and said with a smirk,
"Dashed attractive, some of these Arabs when they're
young. No wonder Lawrence had such a ball out here."

"I wouldn't know." Toby pierced him with a contemptuous, cold blue eye.

"Oh? Not your thing?" Carter was totally indifferent to
his disapproval. "Did you want to see me about something?"

Toby pulled himself together. "Yes. As I mentioned
yesterday, Valerie Pierson has indicated she is coming down
here. I think that would be extremely inadvisable just now,
so I was going to ask you to use what influence you might
have with her to prevent it. In view of what has just
happened, I imagine you are just as anxious as I am to
keep her away from here."

"Look here, what exactly are you hinting at, Glendower?" Carter's voice was suddenly harsh. "Are you
suggesting some *romantic* involvement with Valerie? If
so, I think it is in the most frightful taste—damned scan-
dalous in fact, particularly just now. Val and I are good
friends, that's all."

"Indeed!" Toby murmured, wondering how Valerie
would have reacted to that statement. "Well, I received
the distinct impression last night that the news of her im-
minent arrival was unwelcome to you. If I was mistaken,
then there is nothing further to be said."

"No, you're quite right," Carter said hastily, "I don't
think it would be a good idea at all—terrible memories for
her and all that. In fact, if you think it would help, I can
take a run up to Jerusalem this afternoon and try and talk
her out of it. After all, with the Bedouin under lock and
key, no reason the poor old girl shouldn't buzz off to
England now and start picking up the pieces."

"Ah yes, the handy Bedouin!" Toby said sarcastically.
"How fortunate for everyone here that they were in the
vicinity and so easily caught—even before the results of
the autopsy are out."

"What's that got to do with it?" There was a sharpness
to Carter's tone. "What difference will that make?"

Toby shrugged. "Until it is out I can't say, but I think
it will make quite a lot of difference—yes, quite a lot."

Carter stared at him uneasily. "You think there is some link between the Bedouin and this camp?"

"Possibly," Toby agreed and waited.

Carter continued to stare at him as if trying to read his thoughts, then lowered his voice confidentially. "You know, you may be right. I was going to mind my own business and not say anything, but there is something fishy going on around here. I think Ali may be mixed up in it. He has been slipping out of camp at night. I've seen him several times—the day you arrived for one."

"Oh, and which direction did he go in?"

Carter frowned. "He never seems to go in any one direction. Once it was up there . . ." He jerked his head toward the towering cliffs behind them. "Another time I was putting the old bus away in the wadi below and I saw him sneaking off along the road toward Engedi. To tell you the truth, I wondered even then if he didn't know where old Bill had gone off to, but . . ." He paused and shook his head. "It's not a nice thought when you think he was supposed to be such a friend of his. Still, if you're snooping around you might bear it in mind." Again there was a faint sneer in his voice.

"Indeed I will," Toby agreed, then said pointedly, "If you are going to Jerusalem, hadn't you better be getting off?"

"I suppose I had." He did not sound too enthusiastic at the thought. "Oh, and if you are going to snoop in my tent, do be a good chap and put everything back where you found it. I've got some jolly interesting picture books that ought to titillate the old glands. Be my guest!" And with a sneering laugh he turned his back and walked away.

Toby's fists clenched in fury as the overwhelming, primitive desire to punch John Carter's teeth down his throat swept over him, but with a supreme effort he controlled himself and stalked off toward the site still seething with blind rage. There the peaceful, familiar scene soothed him: the basket boys ambling with their loads to the great sieves by the dump; the metallic click of spades and the short picks of the workmen in the neatly laid out squares; the drowsy murmur of voices. He drew a deep breath of the clear, dry desert air and felt calm return.

Hedecai was sitting on the edge of the scriptorium

quadrant, busily drawing a section, and as he headed for her, Robert Dyke's head popped out of another trench, his face liberally streaked with its dust. "Hi there, Professor!" he called out. "Are we going out again? I'm ready when you are."

"Not today; maybe tomorrow. I have to go into Jericho again to make a call, so there isn't time today. Want to come along?"

"Sure!" Robert grinned engagingly up at him. "My first visit to the bright lights since I got here. Can Hedecai come too?"

"If she wants to."

"Hed!" Robert called out. "Want to come into Jericho and live it up a little later on? I'll stand you a beer."

The chunky girl looked up, nodded, grinned and went back to her work. "Right then," Toby said, his amiability now fully restored. "As soon as work stops for the day. Where's Tahir?"

"Still in the cistern, I think. I've got a really neat bit of wall coming out here. See you," Robert said and popped back into his hole.

As Toby's knoblike head peered over into the deep cistern Tahir spotted it and came up the narrow steps running down one side of it in a series of agile bounds. He was still looking harassed and asked anxiously, "You have seen Mrs. Pierson, you have told her about me?"

"Not yet," Toby said guiltily. In the press of other events, his promise to Tahir had gone clean out of his mind. "But don't worry, I will. All will be well. Is there anything new?"

Tahir looked glumly around. "No. We are very short-handed, as you can see. Goldsmith-*bey* has gone to Jerusalem as you asked. No sooner did he go than Ali went off with Grayson, I do not know where. The new people have not come today, and now Carter-*bey* has not returned. Y'Allah, what can be accomplished when no one works?"

"He has gone to Jerusalem, too, to see Mrs. Pierson," Toby explained, and to prevent a further indignant outburst from the big foreman added hastily, "Tell me, what do you know of that basket boy over there?"

Tahir looked in the direction of the gracile Arab youth. His lip curled and he spat expertly into the dust at Toby's feet. "He is exactly what he looks, *effendi,* the camp whore. Why do you ask?"

"Is he one of those you were talking about earlier, the ones who were giving trouble?"

"Him!" Tahir laughed in scorn. "No! That one makes trouble only as a woman does. He would not be involved in the affairs that concern men. I have the troublemakers right here where I can see them." He nodded his head at the two in the cistern and one who was working in a nearby quadrant. "And they make no trouble when I am around." He curled a hamlike fist significantly. "You have come to work, Glendower-*bey?*"

"Yes, why not," Toby agreed with sudden relief, and ambling over to the scriptorium quadrant, he spent the rest of the afternoon doing what he did best, all thoughts of murder and mayhem firmly banished from his mind.

Later, feeling very much like a schoolmaster on a school outing, he deposited his two charges, who were both in the wildest of good spirits, outside the one café on the main street of Jericho that had disco music blaring from it. He exhorted them, sternly enough he hoped, to meet him there no later than ten thirty and to try to stay out of trouble until then. His duty done, he then went in thankful search of a quieter spot where he could make his call to Penny.

No sooner had he got through to her than she exclaimed excitedly, "Just give me your number there and I'll call you right back. I've asked the manager to use his private phone for reasons you'll soon understand, and what I have to say will take a long time so I'll have to put it on my bill here. This is no time to get cut off through lack of change."

He waited impatiently until the phone shrilled again and then pounced. Penny meant what she said, for her end of it took a solid hour as she reeled off the exhausting and exciting burden of her day. Toby's sole contribution to the conversation was an occasional grunt to let her know he was still there. "So you see," she wound up, "that someone else, the prospective buyer, also must have known about the treasure hunt, and if that buyer is Vadik and he's the murderer, you could be in an awful lot of danger, Toby. I do wish you'd at least let Inspector Abrams in on what you've got so far and let him deal with it."

"Abrams deals with facts," Toby said with some asperity, "and so far I have hardly any facts to give him. Besides, the buyer might *not* be Vadik; it might be Grayson."

"Grayson!" Penny's voice almost broke the phone as it soared into the upper notes of the soprano scale. "But Bill *hated* Grayson. What makes you think a crazy thing like that?"

"Not so crazy. Money makes strange bedfellows. I have still been unable to explain Grayson's presence here, and I do know his name has been linked with several shady antiquities deals in the past. To my mind he is a far more likely middleman for a sale such as this than Vadik. There is also the fact that he seems definitely linked with Ali, who was Bill's right-hand man. The trouble is I think there is more than one thing going on at the site . . ." and he related to her the Arab troubles and the strange episode of the Vadiks. "If Gregory Vadik is an agent, he may be involved with some Arab terrorist plot. After all, it is very much in the Communist interest to keep things stirred up in this area. Those Arabs this morning were angry men. What if something was being planned and Bill's murder has drawn untimely official notice to this area? That would explain their anger."

"But in that case why doesn't Vadik just clear out until things calm down?"

"Just what I warned him to do."

"You *warned* him? Oh, Toby, how could you be so stupid? Why, in heaven's name?" Penny's voice was almost a wail.

"I think Mrs. Vadik is a very nice woman," Toby said gruffly. "I want him to get her out of here."

"But you could be completely wrong," Penny spluttered. "And now you've put him on the alert. Abrams said also that big-money interests might be behind him. If so, he could be the buyer *and* the murderer."

"Then why should Arabs threaten him?" Toby demanded. "That's it, you see; we are still dealing in too many ifs and maybes. I've just got to find out more."

At the other end of the phone, Penny tried to calm herself down because she was now thoroughly alarmed. "Look, Toby, now that you know the Jesus document is genuine and Bill's reputation safely protected, why don't you at least come up to Jerusalem and tell Abrams what you've got thus far? Then if the murderer is at the camp and knows what you have done, there will be no sense in harming you."

"Naturally I'm delighted with Edwards's news," Toby said slowly, "but I think I'd rather wait until Maisler gets his results too. For one thing it'll get Edwards into trouble. For another, the sample we sent to the States was extremely small and I'd like to have it doubly confirmed. Also, with this new information you've got from Miss Cochran—which is extremely valuable, by the way—I can now see something else. One more trip to the desert should confirm it, and then I'll be in a position to give Abrams something concrete."

"Well, tell *me* then!" Penny begged.

"There's no point and no time," Toby said, becoming belatedly aware that there was now a sizable line waiting to use the phone. "It wouldn't mean anything to you, and tomorrow I can tell you for certain. I'll call you at this same time. By the way, how did you get on with persuading Valerie?"

"I haven't been able to find her," Penny snapped. "Whenever I tried her room she was out, and I've been so busy coping with Margaret Cochran, who's a real mess, and running your errands, I haven't had the time to track her down."

"Well, got to go now," Toby said hastily. "Keep on trying. You've been doing great work—keep it up!" and he hung up.

He treated himself to a leisurely dinner accompanied by a choice bottle of hideously expensive imported wine, and then collected his slightly inebriated charges, who, judging by their giggling on the way home, had had a thoroughly good time.

He noted as they drew up on the camp site that all the wanderers had returned. The Vadik camper, the Land Rover and the Jeep were all back in their respective parking places, and as the students giggled off into the darkness, Toby suddenly realized that there was light streaming from the flap of his own tent.

Armed with a wrench from the Jeep, he crept cautiously up and peered around the flap into the lighted interior. Someone was sitting on the camp cot staring blankly at the picture of Bill Pierson. It was Valerie.

CHAPTER 16

"Wait! You haven't told me what you've been doing," wailed Penny into the dead phone, but when she realized that Toby had hung up on her, she slammed it down in a fury. "Of all the insufferable, stubborn *idiots!*" she fumed. "I've a good mind to blow the whistle on him. It would only be for his own good."

Her hand went to the phone again and she began to dial the number Abrams had given her. In the middle she suddenly stopped and cradled the phone; no, she could not do that to him, at least not yet. Memories of Toby gallantly, if complainingly, covering up for her with official-dom as she skittered along her own devious ways flooded over her and her anxious anger died. "No, I can't do it. I've got to give him the same chances he has given me. Another day; I'll wait another day."

There came a light tapping on the door and she opened it on the indignant face of the manager, who evidently had been lurking outside. "Have you finished?" he asked pointedly. "I would like my office back, if you don't mind."

"Oh, certainly!" Penny smiled ingratiatingly. "Most kind of you to have let me use it. I am greatly impressed by your courtesy and kindness."

"There is a message here for you." He sounded molli-fied. "I did not want to interrupt you, but I think it re-quires an immediate answer."

In her jumpy state this instantly filled her with alarm, but it was only a telephone message from Angela Red-ditch, her former student, asking Penny to join her and her diplomat husband for dinner at Pfefferberg's on Yaffa Street at eight o'clock. Penny took a look at the wall clock above the desk. "Goodness, I'll have to hurry!" she gasped, and after a quick call fled to her room for a quick change, postponing once more her search for Valerie.

* * *

"What an extremely nice idea this was, and so very kind of you," Penny remarked with a satisfied sigh as she relaxed after an excellent dinner, to which she had done ample justice.

Her hostess, Angela Redditch, let out a shrill little laugh. "We are delighted you could come—*so* exciting to be mixed up in this *murder* business!" She had been a large, heavy-boned girl who had turned into an even larger, high-colored woman while retaining an early and unfortunate tendency to be kittenish and to talk in emphatics. "You must tell us *all* about it."

"Well, I am not directly involved in this one," Penny said cautiously, "but I did appreciate the information you gave me on John Carter, and would doubly appreciate anything your husband could add." She looked questioningly over at Henry Redditch, who had sat mainly in a good-humored silence during the reminiscent chitchat that had continued through the meal.

He was a rather solemn young man, his pink, shining cheeks looking as if they had only just emerged from a barber's ministrations. Despite the warmth he was clad in a heavy worsted three-piece suit, complete with striped shirt and Harrovian tie, and looked every inch, if somewhat uncomfortably, the English diplomat abroad. He cast a reproachful glance at his wife, who immediately giggled again, then he gave a diffident little cough and said, "It was rather naughty of Angela to gossip to you, Dr. Spring, and I think you can see it would put me in a rather difficult position to talk about a fellow officer except in the most general of terms."

Penny decided to humor him. She put on her most serious expression and replied in a hushed voice, "Of course. I thoroughly appreciate your concern. And I would not dream of asking if it were not such a serious matter. My colleague, Sir Tobias Glendower"—she had already gathered that young Henry liked titles—"is anxious to, er, clear the ground, as it were, before the Israeli authorities become too involved in this, and he is certain they soon will be. Naturally, anything you tell me will be in the strictest confidence and will only be passed on to him. As a Britisher, he is as anxious to protect British interests as you are, and since Carter has hinted to him

that he is here on official business, he is doubly concerned."
She threw this last morsel as deliberate bait, and her fish
rose to it.

Henry Redditch looked faintly shocked and, leaning
forward, murmured confidentially, "I am afraid that is
far from the truth, Dr. Spring. In fact, quite the opposite
of the truth. My information is that Carter has been
'rusticated' pending an investigation. In other words he
has been relieved of all official duties for the moment and
sent on an indefinite leave of absence."

"Couldn't that just be a cover story?" Penny probed.

"No, almost certainly not. In fact this is the second
time it has happened in the past five years." Henry was
warming to his subject. "He was cleared of any active part
in the first case, which happened in East Africa, but was
passed over for promotion. Even if he is cleared this
second time, it is almost certain that he will not be pro-
moted again, and this will mean forced retirement."

"And that will mean a lower pension, and Mr. Carter is
a man of expensive tastes, I believe," Penny said.

"That is his reputation," Henry returned primly.

"Does he have private means?"

He gave a rueful little laugh and shook his head. "Oh,
no! But how many of us have in these sad days?"

"And his expensive tastes run heavily to the ladies?"

"That's not exactly the way I heard it," Henry blurted
out and went a little pink.

"Why, what do you mean, Henry?" his wife piped up.
"I thought you said . . . ?"

"I think Dr. Spring understands what I mean," he cut
her off, and going even pinker, shut his mouth in a firm
line.

Penny knew what he meant and it was a distinct surprise, but, filing it at the back of her mind for further
mulling, she plugged on. "And this trouble he had in East
Africa, could you tell me more about that?"

He shook his head. "I'm afraid that is official business
and I cannot discuss it."

Feeling she had pumped this particular well about as
far as she could, she added, "Does the name Vadik mean
anything to you?"

Looking a little bewildered at this sudden change of subject, he answered, "No, not a thing."

"How about Grayson?"

"No, never heard of him." He looked around and signaled to the hovering waiter for the check.

Penny took the hint. "Well, I really can't thank you enough for all this. It has been very informative and so nice to catch up on all your news." She beamed at Angela. "Perhaps you would be my guests for dinner sometime this week. This is such a nice restaurant!"

"Oh, that would have been lovely, but I'm afraid we won't be here," Angela exclaimed in her incongruous little-girl's voice. "We're off on a VIP trip with the delegation very shortly. Very special!"

"Angela!" her husband said warningly.

"Oh, don't be so stuffy, darling!" she reproved. "Dr. Spring isn't about to go shouting it all over Jerusalem!" She leaned forward confidingly. "It's part of our own little British effort at detente with the Israelis. We'll be trotting around all sorts of important things in the Dead Sea area, and we'll be near Masada. I do hope they take us to see the ruins—*so* exciting!"

"Angela!" Henry repeated on a rising note; she rolled an expressive dark eye at Penny, giggled and fell silent.

As they drove her back to the hotel, in between the inconsequential chitchat about Jerusalem and the potentialities of shopping in the Holy City, Penny began to mull over what she had garnered.

Toby had been right; Carter was in a mess. His career was on the rocks and his financial future grim; a desperate situation. But where did Valerie fit in? If Carter was homosexual, as Henry Redditch had implied, Margaret Cochran had been either dead wrong or lying about him and Valerie. Yet from her own observation she could have sworn there was something going on between them; insofar as she was capable of it, Valerie always glowed at the very mention of his name. So, a one-sided love affair? And Carter presumably with his eye on Valerie's money. Except that Valerie no longer appeared to have any. Oh, dear, Penny sighed inwardly, what a mess it all is! Maybe that is why she's so desperate to get Bill's insurance. In order to hang onto her dubious lover, she has to come up with something fast. I wonder if she knows how much trouble she is in for. She debated whether she should have another go at Margaret Cochran, but decided it was too late. After saying a rather absentminded thank you and good night to the Redditches, she clumped up the stairs of the hotel, but instead of making for her own room went along the passage to Valerie's. "I don't care if she is asleep," Penny muttered. "I think it is time for a little heart-to-heart."

She tapped softly on the door. There was no answer. She tapped louder until a sleepy head popped out from the room next door, growled threateningly at her and popped back in. Penny gave up. "Where the hell is she?" she fretted as she went back to her own room, then stopped, her heart thumping.

Leaning against her door, smoking a thin black cheroot and flicking a lighter nervously on and off, was a very tall, red-haired man with a very disagreeable expression. Penny became acutely aware of the silence of the sleeping hotel and her own small size. Keeping at a safe distance, she managed to get out, "Who are you? What are you doing here?"

The gangly figure came to an upright position and peered down at her in the dim light of the corridor. "Dr. Spring? I'm Selwyn Grayson, and I've been waiting for you for hours." He made it sound like a personal affront.

"What do you want?"

"I've been trying to get in touch with Mrs. Pierson. Nobody here seems to know where she is, but the manager said you might know. I am very anxious to speak with her. Could you come to my room and discuss it?"

"Your room! You're staying here?"

"Just overnight—a friend from the dig will be picking me up tomorrow." Although they were speaking in low tones, his voice had a penetrating, rasping quality which carried all too well, for yet another door opened and a large man clad in gaily striped pajamas came out, glared at them, pointed at his watch, snarled something unintelligible and went back in again, slamming his door.

Quickly deciding between two evils, Penny concluded she'd rather maneuver on home ground, so she whispered, "You'd better come into mine."

She let them in, indicated the sole chair to Grayson and seated herself well away from him on the opposite side of the bed. "Now," she said, "I must say I find this rather surprising, Dr. Grayson. Why are you so anxious to find Valerie?"

His cold gray eyes fixed on hers momentarily, then skittered away. "I wanted to see if there was anything I could do to help her out. It's a bad scene and a bad time for her."

"Admirable but scarcely urgent," Penny commented. "And, in view of the past, rather amazing."

He frowned at her and shifted uneasily on his chair. "Just because Bill Pierson and I had our differences in the past is no reason not to extend a helping hand to Valerie. I've never had anything against her."

"I think there must be something more to it than that," Penny said firmly, "and unless you are a little more frank with me, I'm afraid I can't help you."

He debated in silence for a moment. When he spoke, it was the last thing that Penny expected to hear and took her breath away. "It's the site," he said simply. "It looks as if it is going to be a worthwhile effort after all. I was going to ask her to sign Bill's permit over to me. It can be done—I've already checked with the authorities—but it will need her permission since she financed part of it. I've already talked it over with Goldsmith, who is agreeable to it. I'm ready to make it up to her financially. We've heard she is planning to come down to Wadi Mugharid. Well, neither of us wants her down there, poking around and putting her oar in just when it is becoming interesting."

Another one for the keep-Valerie-away movement, Penny thought; that makes it practically unanimous.

"I hope to persuade her not to come," he went on. "I expect she will be busy with the authorities and Bill's burial arrangements anyway, and I hope she'll be glad about my offer. But first I've got to find her. Where is she?"

"That I don't know." Penny was bland. "I'm afraid I can't help you. I've been trying to find her myself all day. I can only advise you to get some sleep and in the morning try the police, as I am going to do. If anyone knows, they will. I'm surprised you have not already done that yourself."

He surged to his feet and glared down at her. "You mean you've pumped all this out of me for your own damned curiosity! What kind of busybody are you anyway!"

"A busybody who is interested in solving a murder." Penny sounded a lot calmer than she felt. "And I think you are acting in a very peculiar fashion, Dr. Grayson. So, I fancy, will the police. I also think there is no point in discussing this further, so I bid you good night."

He glared wildly at her for a second, then with a curse slammed out of the door. Penny carefully bolted it behind him and, weak with relief, crawled exhausted into bed.

The next morning she cornered the maid, who, since the incident with Toby, had been positively conspiratorial and friendly. The language barrier remained as firm as ever, but with a mixture of pantomime and the few English words the maid knew, Penny managed to get her message across. She towed the maid to Valerie's room and traced a big query on the door. "Where?"

The maid smiled, nodded and made a flapping gesture with her arms. "Gone—man."

"Man—when?"

The maid pantomimed with Penny's watch that it was yesterday afternoon.

"Man—who?" Penny immediately thought of Carter. "Big, fair?"

The maid shook her head, then a delighted grin appeared and she signaled for writing paper. "Name!" She laboriously scribbled on a piece of paper and held it up to Penny. *"Goldsmit,"* it read.

How very odd. So Myron Goldsmith, who, according to Grayson, was as anxious to keep Valerie away from the site as he was, had collected her and carted her off somewhere. Where and why?

"Not all gone," the maid added, confusing her still more. Seeing her puzzled face, the maid winked, used her passkey and showed Penny that Valerie's two suitcases were still in her room. She mimed a small bag.

"So she left with just a few things. Hmm," said Penny, who did not make anything of that either. "Well, thanks anyway." She pressed a pound note into the maid's hand and went out again, dithering between reporting this latest extraordinary development to Abrams and going to see how Margaret Cochran was faring. The latter won out. Leaving a message at the desk for Valerie in case she reappeared, asking her to stay put until they had talked, Penny set out.

In the interests of speed she took a cab, which turned out to be a mistake. The traffic was so dense that she was forced to abandon it at the Damascus Gate and fight her way on foot through the crowded streets of the Old City.

Reaching the dark doorway, she plunged through into the tranquil courtyard and up the rickety steps to Margaret Cochran's door. She knocked loudly and waited. There was no answer. This time she pounded; again no answer. Seriously alarmed, she tried the handle and it yielded to her touch. She ran in, right through the small living room to the bedroom, and stopped in amazement. Everything was neat and orderly, the bed made and empty. The closets gaped wide open—and empty. Margaret Cochran had gone, bag and baggage. Unbelievingly, Penny checked in the other two rooms, but there was no doubt about it. Margaret Cochran was no longer there, nor were any of her personal belongings. A sound at the door froze her, and she wheeled to see it swing open and a man's figure outlined against the sunlight.

Inspector Abrams stepped into the room and smiled mirthlessly at her. "What are you doing here?" she gasped, all sorts of wild forebodings racing through her mind.

"Looking for you," he said tightly. "I tracked you from the hotel. Something very interesting has just turned up, and you've got a lot of explaining to do, Dr. Spring."

CHAPTER 17

Toby gazed up at the roof of the finds tent, to one corner of which he had been banished, and fretted. He had had another unsettled night and thought with near-nostalgia of the privacy of Bill's tent, which he had begun to think of as his own. Damn Valerie anyway! Just when things were starting to come to a head, the last thing he wanted was to have her around, complicating his life still further. Whether it was actuality or his own overtired nerves, the atmosphere of the camp had changed overnight. There was an air of brooding expectancy about it; a sense of action yet unborn that set his nerve ends tingling.

He sat up on the ramshackle cot and rubbed his hands wearily over his face. What to do? Valerie had been so strange the night before, almost as if she were in a walking dream, but she had become almost hysterical when he suggested that she return to Jerusalem, insisting again and again that he must take her to the place where Bill had been killed. He gathered that the police had spared her the gruesome details of Bill's torture and was not about to further upset her by revealing them himself.

Toby tried to reason with Valerie that there was no point in going to the murder scene, but that drove her to further frenzied appeals, and since the last thing he felt able to cope with was a hysterical female, he half-promised that he would. Well, perhaps that would be the best thing. It would get her out of the camp for the day, safe from whatever danger the amazing Vashti had sensed. It would give him a chance to search for his hypothetical spring and, by tonight, maybe Penny would have news from Maisler and he could safely reveal what he had learned so far without harm to Bill. Yes, he would take her to the desert.

Breakfast was a gloomy affair and ill attended. There was no sign of the Vadiks or of Grayson. Goldsmith was already finished by the time Toby arrived and he left almost immediately, muttering that he had to get the workmen started. Ali was nervous and kept licking his lips and darting furtive glances at the new arrival, and the two students, both suffering from slight hangovers, were uncommonly silent.

Only Carter seemed halfway normal, and even his early-morning heartiness had a hollow ring to it. "Well, what are your plans, Val?" he asked. "Going to give the site the once-over and see what we've been up to?"

She favored him with a soulful glance. "No, Toby is going to show me where it happened," she whispered, a convincing break in her voice.

"Oh, I say! Do you think that's a good idea? I mean, won't you find it upsetting?" Carter protested, frowning at Toby.

"No, I want to, I asked him to. I *must* see," she insisted.

He shrugged resignedly. "Well, if that is what you want. Would you like me to come, too?"

"No, that's very sweet of you, John, but I think I'd rather be alone there. I'm sure you both understand." She stared pensively at Carter. Both men nodded solemnly, neither understanding in the least.

"I've no exact idea when we'll be back," Toby said, "but it should be sometime before dark." He had no intention of letting either of them know about his telephone date with Penny.

"Oh, I should jolly well hope so! I mean, just because they've got *some* of those Bedouin wallahs locked up doesn't mean to say there aren't more of them prowling around out there," Carter protested.

"I think with all the police activity there has been in the area since it happened, the Bedouin will be the least of our problems," Toby replied grimly. "Well, Valerie, shall we get started?"

They drove in silence out of the camp; the morning air had a sparkle to it, borne on a slight tangy breeze coming off the Dead Sea below them, but it did nothing to lift Toby's spirits. A dark line of roiling clouds hung over the Mountains of Moab, and he eyed them with disfavor. "Looks as if we may be in for some rain," he commented.

Valerie was gazing straight ahead, her eyes fixed and unseeing. "Is it far?" she said dully.

"No, about seventeen miles, but it is slow going."

"Do you think Bill had found it? The site, I mean." Her voice was abrupt and hard, and the change in it jarred Toby.

"I think he was definitely onto something," he agreed cautiously. "It is a possibility I'd like to check out today."

"Was the cave a part of it?" she demanded.

"In a way. It's below a marker of some sort that may indicate the entrance to the Garden of Zadok. It is nothing I can be certain about until I have done some more exploring. You don't mind waiting for me in the Jeep, do you? I'm sure it's safe enough now."

"I'll come too!" Her tone was eager. "You don't have to worry about me, I've walked miles over rough country with Bill."

"It will mean quite a bit of climbing," Toby said dubiously; he was torn between the necessity to protect her and his own burning curiosity.

"I used to do a lot of climbing. I'm probably better at it than you are." Her jaw had a stubborn set.

"Oh, very well. Then we may as well head straight for it. I'll take you up to the cave later if you still want to see it."

Having gained her point, Valerie let out a small sigh of satisfaction and fell into another brooding silence.

Not wanting to run the slightest risk of getting stuck in the wilderness with Valerie, Toby parked the Jeep in the main wadi before they arrived at the subsidiary one. He unslung the canteen of water and got down, holding out a helping hand to Valerie.

Her fingers in his were icy, but her eyes shone and she said excitedly, "Is this it?"

"No, we have to walk in quite a way, but I don't want to risk the Jeep's axle." He led the way into the gully, on past the murder cave to the point where the vegetation gave out, and stared upward at the cliff face. With the sun full on it, the action of water on the lower boulders was clearly marked. His eyes roamed up and down the cliff face looking for a likely route up. "We've got to get to the top and follow this fault back," he explained. "It looks to me as if it was at one time a very narrow gully that has been stopped up by earthquakes."

"It would be quite an easy climb straight up," she challenged.

"No, there has to be an easier way." He set off down the barren part of the wadi and soon found a goat path that wound upward. Scrambling and slipping, they toiled until they arrived panting at the top; of the two Valerie appeared the less winded and immediately set off back toward the fissure. Toby shaded his eyes and looked around. From up here the fortress of Masada was clearly visible. The massif on the other side of the wadi behind him was very flat save for the lone pinnacle of rock above the murder cave, which looked even more impressive from this perspective. He looked toward Engedi and saw a small procession of black cars crawling like ants along the Dead Sea road.

Then Valerie's voice summoned imperatively, "Toby, I've found the gully again. Now what do we do?"

Toby joined her and looked into a boulder-filled crevice that was not more than six feet across at the top. "We follow it back into this massif." He walked off, with her close on his heels, and in a few minutes was looking down at a sight that set his pulse pounding. The crack suddenly opened and dipped into a small, deep, oval-shaped valley not more than sixty feet in diameter, with great boulders littering its floor. The far end of the valley was gently rounded into a semicircle like the apse of a church, and at the base of it, clear amid the natural rubble, stood blocks of worked stone: he could even make out the remains of a small fluted column. And behind this rock melange of man and nature he could see dark openings at the bottom of the cliff face. "My God, it's like a miniature Petra—a valley with a hidden entrance!" he breathed.

Valerie clutched at his arm, her eyes bright with excitement. "Is this it?"

"We'll have to get down there and see." He strode off around the perimeter of the oval valley, but scan as he might, there was no discernible way down into it.

"What can we do?" Valerie asked, her voice tight with disappointment.

Toby ruminated. "It looks about seventy feet deep. There's a hundred-foot coil of rope in the Jeep. We'll have to get it and come back. We can hitch it around a boulder up here and I can rappel myself down. You'd better stay up here."

"I can manage just as well as you can," she insisted. "You've no cause to worry about me. I want to see what's there."

Toby was too excited to argue. Rather than retrace their steps they went back along the cliff edge looking for another way down, and this time found a much easier pathway down the cliff, almost opposite to the murder cave. Toby pointed it out to her. "See, the cave is directly underneath that rock pinnacle. Bill must have been working out its significance in locating the garden when he was killed."

"But how did you figure that out?" Valerie demanded.

Toby was in a quandary because he did not want to reveal at this point how he had come by his extra knowledge. "It's very complicated," he said hastily. "I'll give you the full details later, if you like, but now the important thing is to get down into the valley and see if it really *is* what we think, don't you agree?"

She had been gazing up at the cave entrance and said abruptly, "I'd like to go up there for a few minutes by myself. Do you mind? You don't need me to come back to the Jeep with you, do you?"

"No, not at all." Toby was relieved to be briefly rid of her and showed her the pathway up to the rock shelf before setting off at a brisk pace for the Jeep.

"Don't forget to bring something to dig with, too!" she called after him. "And if you don't have a copy of the Copper Scroll directions with you, I have one."

Extraordinary creature! he reflected as he busily packed the rope, a flashlight and some food into a knapsack and gathered up a short-handled spade to add to the collection. He was torn between admiration and revulsion; admiration for her unexpected physical dexterity and endurance, for so far she had not uttered a single word of complaint, and revulsion that the thing uppermost in her mind was so evidently the treasure and not her husband's untimely death. "Still," he muttered, "mustn't be too harsh. After all she wanted to be by herself in the place he spent his last hours, and that shows some feeling. Having a bit of a cry, I imagine." But when he found her waiting for him in the wadi, although she was out of breath and with unaccustomed color in her pale cheeks, there were no signs of tears, shed or unshed, in her eyes, which indeed sparkled with excitement.

They climbed up the cliff face again, Toby in the lead. She lagged behind at the top, and when Toby turned, she was crouching down with her back to him, fiddling with some small rocks. "What are you doing?" he said testily. "If we are going to get anything done before dark, there's no time to lose."

She turned and faced him coolly. "Precisely what I was thinking, so in case we don't get back here until dark, I've marked the pathway down." She stepped aside to reveal the small white square of a handkerchief weighted down by the rocks. "I certainly don't intend to get marooned up here!"

Toby grunted a grudging approval and moved on. Circling the valley again they chose a spot where tumbled boulders formed a giant staircase, and with the rope firmly anchored to a sizable boulder at the top found it easy enough to rappel down from boulder to boulder into the valley below. "It'll be a lot harder going up," Toby grumbled as he reached the valley floor. His leather-soled boots had a tendency to slip on the crumbly surface of the boulders, and he had made heavier weather of the descent than Valerie, who had crepe-rubber soles on hers.

"It'll be no problem with the rope," she returned. "We'll have to climb a bit, but with the good firm handhold it provides it'll be easy. I'll go first and give you a hand-up over the difficult bits." And for once she sounded more comforting than condescending.

He grunted and gazed around. The floor of the tiny valley was thick with yellowish grass, and there were a few sizable bushes growing around the outer perimeter. "Definitely water around here somewhere," he muttered and looked for the telltale seepage of a spring. The cascade of boulders was so great at the end of the valley leading to the blocked gully that it was impossible to make out what went on behind them; however his quick eye picked out a regular line of stones running along the left-hand side of the valley and he knelt and started to dig around them with his trowel, as Valerie watched with silent interest. In a few minutes he got to his feet with a satisfied grunt. "Well, there was a conduit for water built along here"—he sketched a straight line with his trowel—"so I imagine the spring must be hidden somewhere under that pile of rock."

Valerie had got out a sheet of paper and was studying it. "We've got to find the excedras," she muttered absently. "Then all the rest should be easy."

Toby began to take bearings from the compass on his watch. "That's south," he said with mounting excitement, waving a hand toward the apsidal end of the valley where he had seen the broken columns, ". . . and that's east, and there, by George, if I'm not mistaken, is the cistern hollowed out of the rock!" He strode off toward the dark opening that showed at the base of the cliff, Valerie close at his heels. Playing the flashlight down into it, he whistled softly. "That is certainly a deep one—twenty feet or more. I can't even make out the bottom." He chucked in a small rock, which landed with a dull, thumping echo below. "No water in it now, though."

"Surely that's not very important." Valerie was impatient. "There were only bars of silver there. It's the book we have to find."

Toby looked around at her curiously. "Bill told you that, did he?"

She stared back. "How else would I know? The book should have the full instructions for locating all the rest of the Temple treasure. It's worth a king's ransom."

"To whom?" he demanded. "You weren't going to give it to the Israelis, and presumably you weren't going to take it yourselves and start digging little holes all over Israel. Who was going to buy it when you found it?"

She stared at him, her thin lips pressed so firmly together that they almost disappeared. "I don't know; he didn't tell me."

Toby was certain she was lying but was not about to press the point. "Well, it's all pretty academic now anyway," he said and moved off toward where he had seen the fallen pillars.

"What do you mean?" Valerie came after him.

He did not answer but knelt down and said excitedly, "Look! Traces of marble paving, and that's a scrap of portico and here are some fragments of broken pilasters. By God, this *is* the excedra!"

She swung around. "So the tomb should be behind us somewhere. What should we look for?"

Toby got up again, then froze. "Did you hear that?" he demanded.

"No, what?" She glanced uneasily up at the cliffs over their heads.

"I thought I heard a stone rattle down over there."

"I didn't hear anything. Probably we loosened some on our way down."

He stood listening intently, but there was nothing further. "I suppose so." He paced off a few strides due north from the edge of the marble paving and stopped with a rueful laugh. Facing them was a pile of tumbled boulders, all of considerable size and weight. "So much for Zadok's tomb! It will take a squad of strong men to move those."

"You're sure it's the right place?" There was dismay in her voice.

"The instructions are not specific, but yes—if this is the site of Zadok's tomb, that is just where it should be." He knelt down again and started to ferret around beneath the boulders. "There are some scraps of broken marble here, too. Chances are the tomb itself was demolished by the rockfall. In any case it will be no problem for the Israelis. They could even remove the boulder debris with an electric winch."

"What do you mean—the Israelis?" There was a quiver in her voice.

He glanced grimly up at her. "There is no point in keeping this secret any longer, Valerie. Bill is dead, and the whole scheme was pretty wild anyway. As soon as we get back, I'll inform the authorities. And don't worry about Bill's reputation; there is something I haven't told you yet, but he won't suffer a bit from this, I promise you. And with that out of the way, I can also promise you that I shall shortly be able to give the police his murderer."

"Oh, indeed! That's interesting, very interesting," she said with a curious inflection, "but it won't do, Toby. I'm afraid it just won't do . . ."

He sensed a sudden movement behind him and started to get up, half turning as he did so. "What?" he began to say, but at that instant the world exploded into blinding pain and he went toppling forward into darkness.

"Is he dead?"

"Not yet, but he soon will be. Give me a hand with him over to the cistern."

"You heard?"

"Yes, enough." There was a dull, crunching thump as Toby's inert body was pushed over into the dark depths.

"Oh, dear, I don't like this. Did you have to do it so soon? How shall I explain?"

"You won't have to. He found the site; that is all that matters. And if anyone ever finds him, the death will be ruled accidental from the fall."

"But I don't understand—if I go back without him . . ."

"You aren't going back." There was savage amusement in the man's voice as his hands seized Valerie's throat from behind. There was the beginning of a strangled scream which stirred the echoes in the sleeping valley, and then the thin neck snapped like a twig and the pale head flopped lifelessly sideways. "He served his purpose and you yours." The man chuckled, and with a quick heave sent her body tumbling into the depths of the cistern. "You can keep each other company in hell."

This done, he picked up the discarded knapsack and canteen, slung them over his shoulder and stood looking around with an air of pride. "Half a million," he murmured, "and cheap at the price. So perish all my enemies!" Then, silent as he came, he made his way out of the hidden valley, coiling up the rope behind him. When he got to Valerie's pathetic little marker, he removed that too. "Good thinking, Mrs. Pierson, but only the buyer will ever know," he mused, and chuckled again. "Someone will certainly be in for a surprise down there. Still, *caveat emptor!* Now there is just one little detail left to take care of. . . ." And, humming to himself, he made his way down to the wadi below.

CHAPTER 18

"I believe in America the term is 'laying it on the line.' " Abrams's smile was pleasant but his voice was hard. "And that is just what I am going to do, and if you have the intelligence you are credited with, you will do the same. Otherwise you and Sir Tobias will be in very serious trouble."

"I'm extremely worried about Miss Cochran," Penny said desperately, hoping to sidetrack him. "Last night she was in a very overwrought state, and now this disappearance . . ."

Abrams waved a dismissive hand. "I've already put out a bulletin to locate her. If she is still in Israel, she'll be found and brought in, or if she has left the country, we'll know where she has gone. That, at the moment, is of minor concern. What concerns me, what has concerned me all along, is why Dr. Pierson was tortured before he was killed. There had to be a motive, and I think you know that motive and a lot more besides about what has been going on at Wadi Mugharid."

He paused and looked gravely at her. "A very interesting piece of information has come into my hands. It is from a shady dealer in antiquities who, for reasons of his own, is anxious to be on good terms with the police. He reports that several days ago a young Arab came into his store with a piece of paper he wanted translated. The Aramaic had been garbled by whoever had transcribed it and the dealer could make little sense of it. What he did make out led him to believe that someone had transcribed it from an ancient scroll. He pressed the youth about this, saying if he brought the original he could translate it, but otherwise could do nothing. The youth became nervous, snatched the paper back and rushed out of the store, but the dealer was interested enough to watch and saw him talking to what he describes as a tall foreigner. The man is old and does not see clearly, and before the dealer could

163

follow them, they had got into a cab and gone off. None of this would have meant anything had he not remembered some of the content of the paper, which he said was to do with the Garden of Zadok and the Finger of God. It is a singular coincidence, is it not, that you have in your possession an extract from the Copper Scroll about the Garden of Zadok, with *added* notes about the Finger of God? So, Dr. Spring, what about it? I want to know *now* if Sir Tobias has been concealing evidence, and if so, why."

"You don't think *he* was the man the dealer saw, do you?" Penny said indignantly.

"You tell me. Sir Tobias has made quite a point of the fact that he knows little Hebrew *and* that he was alone at the murder site for a considerable period before the police arrived. Not only that. As a matter of course I reported this possible new scroll find to Maisler at the Archaeological Museum. At first he was extremely cagey when Sir Tobias's name was mentioned. Then when I told him the *content,* his whole attitude changed. He became very excited and insisted I go to Wadi Mugharid at once to bring Sir Tobias back. And that, after we have had this little talk, is precisely what I am going to do. I am also going to bring back Mrs. Pierson, who, according to my information is also down there."

The jig was very much up, Penny thought in dismay. "You are quite wrong about Sir Tobias," she said stoutly, "but I can see it is best to tell you everything I know, because for one thing, the tall man the dealer saw is almost certainly the murderer. Those notes you saw of mine did not come from Sir Tobias, they came from Margaret Cochran . . ." and she rapidly sketched out as diplomatically as she could all they had found out thus far, emphasizing the fact that Bill Pierson was after the new site rather than the treasure, and omitting all references to the Jesus document.

Abrams listened patiently and at the end said, "All right, if the tall man was not Sir Tobias, who was he?"

"That's just it—he could be one of several," Penny said with acute anxiety. "Presumably to your informant anyone not an Israeli or an Arab would be a foreigner, so without a clearer description it could be Grayson, Carter, Vadik or even Tahir the foreman!" She went on to tell him what she knew of them. "The last time I talked to Toby he said he thought he was on the right track, but before I could get his latest thoughts he rang off.

"You're right," she continued. "We should go down there at once. Toby told me Vashti Vadik had been very insistent that there was danger both to him and Valerie Plerson, and now you tell me Valerie has already gone down to the site. If Vadik is as dangerous as you say, they may be in serious trouble. Personally I still favor Grayson as the most likely character, and there is no doubt about it that Carter is not as above-board as he seems and was in the best position to know about Bill's discovery . . ." She did not elaborate on that. "But, whoever it is, the main thing is to make sure nothing further happens." She jumped to her feet. "Can we go right now?"

"If you·had told me all this yesterday, Dr. Spring, we might have had the murderer in custody by now," Abrams said severely. "By your untimely silence you may have jeopardized other innocent lives. I only hope it is not already too late." But one look at her worried face showed him he did not have to belabor the point. "Anyway, let's get off . . ."

But suddenly there was an interruption. A young constable came rushing in, saluted smartly and handed over a folded piece of paper to Abrams. "It is very urgent, sir."

Abrams read it and came to his feet with a curse, his face working. "I'm afraid this takes precedence," he said in a choked voice. "Dr. Spring, I will drop you off at Wadi Mugharid with one of my men, but I must go on to Engedi. Officer Baum has just been killed. It seems he was on a routine check ahead of an official party going to the ruins of Masada and his Jeep ran into a terrorist booby trap and exploded. The terrorists were evidently after—"

"Don't tell me! The British delegation to the Knesset," Penny said hollowly. "Oh, my God!"

The heavens opened as the police car hit the level ground beyond Jericho; storm clouds rolled overhead and the placid face of the Dead Sea was obscured by great sheets of rain that swept and scoured the surface like machine-gun fire. It was not so much a rainstorm as a deluge, slowing the police car to a crawl as the driver peered through a dim curtain of rain. Penny sat in numb misery in the back of it, beside the tight-faced inspector. Unable to bear her own thoughts a moment longer, she said, "When I get to the camp, what do you want me to do?"

"To start with, get Sir Tobias to write out a full statement of everything that has happened so far—holding back *nothing*, I might add. And, if you can persuade her, Mrs. Pierson too. But, I may point out, since she evidently is not connected with the crime, that her position in this is not half as equivocal as yours is."

I wish I were sure of that, Penny thought dismally.

"I have no idea how long I will be at Engedi, but with a policeman in the camp, I doubt anything can happen. However, as soon as I get back, I shall be taking all three of you back to Jerusalem. And you may point out to Sir Tobias that I would prefer this to be voluntary, but if necessary I shall place him under arrest."

"Isn't that somewhat extreme?" Penny protested.

"Dr. Spring, you still do not seem to understand. I am *protecting* him. There is a murderer somewhere here, in all probability right in the camp. With the information you have given me, I am now positive that the Bedouin we still have in custody did not murder Dr. Pierson. There is no doubt they robbed and stripped the vehicle—that is beyond question—but I have seen the Arab in the hospital and now believe his story that they found both Pierson's watch and wallet *in* the Jeep. I speak no ill of a dead officer . . ." his voice shook slightly, "but Officer Baum was too precipitate in his assumptions. He honestly believed he had caught a shark when all he had in reality was a bunch of minnows. But, by God, if Vadik is behind this terrorist attack, *this* time he will not escape!"

"So you think he is at the bottom of all this?"

"At this juncture I simply don't know, but I most surely am going to find out." Abrams's voice was like flint. "And to make sure he causes no further trouble, I intend to take him with me for questioning."

They turned onto the track leading up to the plateau, on the edge of which the Vadik camper was dimly visible through the pelting rain. They churned into the sodden camp. After a low-voiced series of orders to one of the police constables, Abrams left with the other and marched over to the camper. Penny was not given the opportunity to see the outcome, for the other policeman opened her door and motioned her out and over to the big tent that stood in the middle of the drab-green encampment like a mother hen surrounded by chicks.

Stumbling through the mud, even in that short distance, they arrived at the mess tent soaked and breathless. They burst in. Penny was too anxious for niceties; scanning the surprised faces seated around the long table and not finding the one she was longing to see, she said abruptly, "Where's Sir Tobias?"

A pale-faced, bespectacled man at the end of the table looked up at her blearily over the edge of a glass and muttered, "Gone—just like all the bloody rest of them—gone. It's finished. I'm finished." He drained his glass.

"What do you mean?" Penny snapped.

An anxious-looking girl, whom she correctly identified as Hedecai, answered, "You mustn't mind Myron; we have had an upsetting morning. Professor Glendower went off with Mrs. Pierson after breakfast. I think he was taking her to where her husband was killed."

"And something has happened to them?" Penny felt her knees begin to shake, so sat down abruptly in the nearest chair.

"Oh, no. They're probably sheltering from the storm. It is just that most of our laborers seem to have decamped overnight and they've taken a lot of things with them. That is why Myron is so upset."

The tent flap opened to admit another figure, and John Carter, his fair hair sleeked down with the rain, came in, mopping his face with a handkerchief. "Whew! It's murder out there!" he announced cheerfully, causing Penny to wince. He took in the newcomers and his eyes widened. "Hello! What's up now? More police?"

"I'm Penelope Spring," Penny said. "I'm most anxious to get in touch with Sir Tobias, and this officer brought me down."

"Oh, I thought I heard a car," he said easily, then gave a rueful laugh. "Well, I'm afraid you're in for a wait. He and Valerie took off this morning, and my guess is that they are right royally stuck somewhere. When I saw this storm coming up, I thought I'd go after them and give them a hand if needed, but it struck too soon and my old bus got stuck on the way back to camp. Had to walk half a mile—got soaked!"

Penny looked anxiously around. "Where is everyone else?"

"Gone!" came Myron's muffled voice from the end of the table.

John Carter looked over at him, shook his head and gave Penny a knowing wink. "Our Myron's feeling a bit under the weather, I see. The Vadiks are in their camper, I suppose. Grayson and Ali must have just got back. Grayson's Land Rover has churned up the ground something shocking. He'll be lucky to move it again. They are in Grayson's tent clucking away like a couple of wet hens."

"You know where Sir Tobias went?"

"Well, only in a general sort of way. I was following their tracks, y'see, until the rain came on."

"Who does know the way?" Penny asked.

"Robert and Tahir the foreman were with him that first time," Hedecai answered.

"You're surely not going to try to go out in this?" Carter put in. "Those wadis will be gushing water by this time. You'd get stuck within a hundred yards."

"As soon as the rain starts to slacken, I must try. It is very urgent," Penny said again. "Where is Robert?"

Hedecai frowned slightly. "He stayed behind at the site to cover up some things when the rain started. He must be in his tent drying off."

A sudden sense of urgency seized Penny. She knew Robert had been with Toby on that second trip when he stumbled onto something. It seemed vital to know what that was. "Would you show me his tent?" she said to Hedecai. "I must talk to him."

"Certainly." They went out into the pouring rain and sloshed over to one of the little tents. "Robert, are you decent? Someone to see you," Hedecai called.

There was no answer and she poked her head around the flap. "Not here—that's funny!" she said in a puzzled voice. "Maybe he's in the finds tent."

An awful foreboding swept Penny. "He was alone at the site?"

"Yes."

"Then quick, take me there!"

They struggled through the mud around the cliff spur to the empty, rain-swept site. "He was putting tarpaulins over the scriptorium and some of the better-preserved mud-brick walls," Hedecai explained. "They wash away so quickly. But he's not here. Where can he have got to?"

"Show me where they were," Penny said desperately.

They sloshed around to no avail until they came to the fourth quadrant. Then Hedecai let out a shrill scream and jumped down into the trench. Lying huddled at the bottom, face down and with the back of his head a nightmare of blood and mud, lay Robert Dyke.

Penny jumped in after her and felt at the cold wrist for the sign of a pulse. It was very faint and thready, but still there. "He's alive! Quickly, go fetch Tahir and the policeman and have them carry him back to the expedition Jeep," she ordered the shocked girl. "We've got to get him to a hospital as fast as we can. You are going to have to explain to the policeman that we have to leave immediately for Jerusalem."

For a moment after Hedecai had raced away, Penny knelt beside the young man and looked at the rock lying beside him covered with blood and hair, a desperate anger at her heart. Then she hurried back to the mess tent.

The unconscious body was tenderly loaded into the Jeep, where Hedecai cradled the mutilated head in her arms. Penny, thanking heaven for small mercies, had no trouble with the policeman, who, after a swift explanation, averred through Hedecai, as Penny took the wheel, that he would not allow anyone in the camp to move an inch before she returned.

Through the slackening rain they sped off again to Jerusalem. "Who would want to do this to Robert?" sobbed Hedecai in the back.

"The murderer of Dr. Pierson," Penny said through gritted teeth.

"But why?" Hedecai wailed.

"Because he is the only one who knows where Sir Tobias was going today," Penny grated, and wished she did not know what that signified. She knew already in her heart that her one hope of seeing Toby alive again lay locked in the battered mind of Robert Dyke. He must not die; he *could* not die.

CHAPTER 19

Toby filtered reluctantly back to consciousness to the sound of drumming, with water running into his mouth and nose. He coughed, choked and tried to sit up, with agonizing results. It was a vain attempt. He was lying face down in a pool of water; his brain felt as if it had been split apart and told him that at least one of his legs and probably both had been broken. "Get up, you fool, or you'll drown," it told him.

With a mighty effort of will and accompanying pain that set his senses swimming, he managed to roll over on his back. Tentatively he flexed his arms; his left shoulder hurt abominably, but otherwise his arms appeared intact. He gazed upward at a patch of grayish light on his right, high up in the blackness. The cistern; he had been pitched into the cistern. Why he had not broken every bone in his body including his neck amazed him, but his questing fingers established that the floor of the cistern was soft and yielding; that and his own limp, unconscious state had saved him. His right hand groped for the wall and found its plastered surface running with little rivulets of water. The storm clouds he had seen were evidently shedding their burden on the wilderness, and he wondered uneasily how deep the water in the cistern would get. He would have to get higher, but how?

His left hand groped into the darkness and drew back in revulsion as it encountered icy flesh. He fumbled in his pants pocket for the small flashlight he always carried. Praying that it would still work, he pressed the button and in the answering tiny stream of light made out the thin body of Valerie Pierson, her head twisted away from him at an impossible angle. His brain absorbed this new shock, collated it and delivered its message.

He could see now with startling clarity. Valerie had set him up. Bill's murderer must have followed behind them,

waited in the murder cave for her to give the all-clear,
then followed the trail she had left for him. Then, once
Toby had established the site, he had struck and, after
dealing with Toby, he had turned on his partner and dealt
with her as ruthlessly as he had with everyone else. "Never
mind," Toby comforted the still figure, "he won't get
away with it, Valerie!"

The most disturbing thought that came to him was that
he would have to share this bizarre prison with her until
succor, in the shape of Penny, arrived. He never for one
moment doubted that she would, but how long would it
take her? Now let me see, he ruminated, when I don't call
tonight, she'll come down to see what's up. She'll find out
that I went to the murder cave with Valerie, will contact
young Robert, who knew roughly what I had in mind to
do, and will zero on that. She'll check the wadi, find traces
of the spring, which *should* be in operation after this deluge, and that will be that. Hmm. At best twenty-four hours
and at worst forty-eight. Well, I can last that long. At
least, if I don't drown, I won't die of thirst.

He lay there pondering how he could get some signal
out of the cistern onto the valley floor until the deepening
water once more began to trickle into his mouth, forcing
him into action. Fortunately the chill of it was numbing
his legs, so levering himself up by his arms, he swung
himself around so that his back was propped against the
cistern wall. He began to play the flashlight around to take
full stock of his prison.

The cistern was about ten feet long and eight feet wide.
Unfortunately it was also about twenty feet deep, and
with both his legs out of action . . . "Even if I got out of
this, I could never get out of the valley," he mused. "Still,
it *would* be much easier to set up a signal if I were outside." Since no immediate solution to that problem leapt
into his mind, he contented himself with doing little sums
concerning the volume of the cistern. Unless the rain continued for a very long time, he would be in no danger of
drowning. "I suppose that's some comfort," he told his
brain, "but I wish you'd get busy on the other problem.
I've got to get out of here."

The act of sitting up had had a negative effect on his
concussed head. He was beset by blinding flashes and balls

of color streaming in from the periphery of his vision and exploding in aching cascades behind his eyeballs. He found it easier to keep his eyes closed and let the process go on internally; after a while the explosions tapered off into blackness.

He woke up to find that he had slumped forward face down into the water again. "This will never do," he chided himself, and so once more propelling himself by his arms, dragging his useless legs behind him, he painfully worked his way to the nearest corner of the cistern and wedged himself into it. "You see, class," he babbled to a phantom audience, "this is an elementary precaution to take in these particular circumstances. Note that, for now, if I become unconscious, I shall not fall sideways or forward. Also I am in a better position to throw things out of the opening." The fireworks display started up again, spinning, whirling, exploding, until the merciful veil of blackness once more descended and he slept.

With every hour that passed, Penny's frantic anxiety mounted, and in consequence she was making a thorough nuisance of herself. Only Abrams, who understood what demons of guilt tormented her, had any patience, and that was wearing a little thin. With daylight the storm had passed, and a helicopter scanning the area for traces of the terrorist gang had rapidly spotted the deserted Jeep. But there the trail had ended. A party spearheaded by Tahir had searched the wadi, the caves, the whole area to no avail: Tobias Glendower and Valerie Pierson had vanished without a trace.

Robert Dyke had been operated on at the Hadassah Hospital in Jerusalem, where he still lay unconscious though out of danger. The doctors had found a depressed fracture of the skull. Abrams realized grimly that the young man, having been struck down from behind, probably would not even know who had tried to kill him. Penny had quarreled with both doctors and nurses in her frenzied attempts to stay at his bedside and had been banished from the hospital. Only Abrams's official intercession had persuaded them to allow Hedecai to stay with the unconscious youth, primed with all the questions Penny knew must be answered when he came around. This might be in a few days or a few weeks, the doctors opined, for there was no telling how much the brain had been damaged.

Meanwhile the official interrogation at the camp continued without mercy. Carter and Goldsmith had already called loudly for the British consul, Grayson for the American, and the whole situation·was blowing up into an international incident. The shaken British parliamentary delegation had been shepherded out of the wilderness under tight military security, and throughout, Gregory Vadik, who had called for no one, blandly parried all attempts to break him down. Two days passed thus, and things were at an impasse.

"You've *got* to extend the search," Penny begged.

Abrams, who privately believed the missing pair were already beyond mortal aid, said patiently, "The search *is* going on, but you must realize that it would take a whole army months to search every corner and cave in the Judean Wilderness. We are doing what we can, but all we can hope for is a break."

By the third day Penny was clutching at straws, so when Vashti Vadik asked to see her, she leaped at the chance.

Vashti had not escaped the attention of the police. Her thin face was pinched and there were great dark circles under her green eyes as she said in an exhausted voice, "I want to help. I really do. The police keep trying to make me say things I cannot say, but I must find the professor and all will be well. It must be soon, soon."

"You can tell me anything," Penny said eagerly. "I won't tell them."

"You have something of the professor's, something personal he has given you? I must have it."

Penny's face fell. "No, I don't. Wait! I may have something." She dumped out the entire contents of her bag and scrabbled through it, coming up with a torn page from Toby's notebook. "Will this do?"

"If it is all you have, it will have to." Vashti took it and pressed it against her forehead. She shivered and closed her eyes. "Dark! Wet! Oh!" She clutched at her leg. "Such pain! Throw, throw, throw . . ."

"He's alive!" Penny prompted.

"Yes, but there is death with him; near, so near. He must get out."

"Yes, but where, *where?*"

"A hidden place." Vashti's face contorted with pain. "Great rocks . . . a valley . . . oh, I cannot see!" Then a relieved look came over her. "But there is a great white light surrounding him in the darkness. He is protected. We may still have time!" She opened her eyes and smiled.

"Is that *all?*" Penny cried in the disappointment of despair.

Vashti's thin hand clutched hers. "He is protected. There is still time. You must have faith!"

On the second day Toby's fever had mounted as rapidly as the level of the water in the cistern had fallen. He had scooped mud and buried Valerie's body in a cocoon of it; Bill had come and been a great help to him. "We both forgive you, Valerie," he babbled.

On the third day Bill went away, but the company got even more interesting. He had a long talk with Judas Iscariot about his motives for the betrayal, and an equally long one with Joseph of Arimathea about the real location of his tomb. Then they went away and Jesus of Nazareth came. Toby was not at all surprised at this; to him it made a lot of sense. In the days when the Essene community at Wadi Mugharid had flourished, the Garden of Zadok must have been a green and blooming spot, a spot for a pleasant pilgrimage into the wilderness; here they must have come for a respite from the bare and burning hills.

"I'm afraid I am getting rather weak," Toby confessed to the slight figure. "I thought I had better mention it, because I am not sure how much longer I can hang on and I have got to get out of here."

"I can take away your pain," he was assured. "The rest is up to you. You must have faith. . . ."

"Dr. Spring!" Hedecai's voice over the phone was breathless with excitement. "Robert is conscious! He's very weak, but I think he understood what I was saying. It doesn't make any sense to me, but maybe it will to you. He says to go up the wadi until the vegetation stops. There is a big crack in the wall. It is something to do with a spring. The professor was going to follow it back to see where it led. Something about a garden?"

"The Garden of Zadok?"

"Oh, so that is what he was trying to say. Yes, I think so."

"Right!" Penny felt a brief surge of hope. "I'll go right away," she said, and hurried to find Inspector Abrams.

"We'll go by helicopter," he decided. "It'll save time."

"Vashti Vadik must come too," Penny said urgently. "I believe she'll be more use than all the rest of us. It has been four days. Even if they are alive they may be in such poor shape they'll not be able to signal."

Abrams was so tired and frustrated he did not even argue; the search for the terrorists had yielded nothing, the interrogation at the camp had yielded nothing. He too was ready to clutch at any straw.

The two small women and four large policemen were packed into the large Army helicopter he had commandeered, and they whirled off to the wilderness. The pilot set them neatly down on the massif almost opposite the murder cave, and Penny scurried along the edge of the cliff, gazing anxiously down into the wadi below. She was so intent on what she was doing that when she came to the break in the cliff, she almost fell into it and was restrained only by Abrams's saving hand. They raced in silence along its sinuous course, the helicopter hovering over them like a giant dragonfly, until the oval concavity of the valley appeared.

Vashti clutched at Penny. "Yes, yes, see! The valley, the great rocks! Yes, he is near!"

Abrams stood at the edge and gazed dubiously down into the depths. "I very much doubt they are here—how would they ever get down? You can see at a glance there is no path from the top."

Penny had grabbed his field glasses and was scanning the floor of the valley. "I don't care; we've got to go down and search. Look, there are caves over there! Vashti said a dark place."

He threw an exasperated glance at the thin figure, her black hair streaming in the wind off the Dead Sea. Vashti had her eyes screwed up in desperate concentration as she peered around the valley floor. Suddenly her hand shot forward. "Over there by that cave opening," she cried. "I see something glinting on the ground."

They ran around the valley's rim until they were above the spot she had indicated. Penny focused in with the glasses. "It's a pencil," she exclaimed, "a gold pencil! And there's something beside it. It's a notebook! Toby's black notebook!" She choked with excitement.

Abrams got out his walkie-talkie. "Can you set her down in the valley?" he asked the helicopter pilot.

"Not a chance. I'd smash her up."

"Then set down here and we'll get the equipment." The dragonfly settled beside them, and in minutes stretchers, nets and slings were littering the valley's edge and coils of rope were snaking into the valley below.

"Toby!" Penny called over the edge. "Toby, we're here." Her voice stirred hollow echoes but there was no reply.

"You had better stay here with Mrs. Vadik," Abrams ordered.

"Not on your life!" And before he could stop her, Penny, who had never descended a rope in her life, had hopped over the edge like a chubby monkey and was sliding into the depths. She arrived at the bottom winded and with her hands bleeding from rope burns, but she was too excited even to notice. Abrams reached the valley floor at the same time she did and tried to hold her back from the cistern, whose depths two constables were already probing with flashlights. She broke free, ran to the edge and stopped, appalled.

It was like looking at a nightmare in slow motion. A figure lay prone on the floor of the cistern, the back of its head black with dried blood and caked in gray mud from head to toe. As she watched, the right hand slowly came up grasping a handful of mud and painfully added it to a small ramp of mud built against the cistern wall. The ramp was about three feet high. The hand came back, scrabbled another handful and repeated the process. "Oh, Toby!" she whispered, tears blinding her eyes. "Thank God!"

The policemen scaled down and extracted their feebly moving burden from the cistern. The young police paramedic took over as Penny watched in an agony of suspense. Finally the paramedic straightened up and delivered his verdict to Abrams. "His left leg is broken, the right badly sprained. He's got pneumonia and there's a bad concussion, possibly a fracture. He's pretty weak, but his pulse is as steady as a rock. It is remarkable. If we can get him to the hospital fast, he should be all right. I hope!"

There was a short delay as the helicopter became airborne again. Its hook lowered slowly into the valley as the police readied the stretcher for hoisting. Toby's eyes had been closed when they brought him out of the cistern, but now Penny saw the lids fluttering as if he was fighting back to consciousness. She went over and knelt beside the stretcher, taking his mud-covered hand. "It's me, Toby, It's Penny," she whispered. "You're going to be all right, but tell me if you can: do you know who the murderer is?"

The lids did not open, but the cracked and swollen lips parted and the mouth worked. "Of course I do," croaked Sir Tobias Glendower before he slipped away once again into painless oblivion.

CHAPTER 20

The final act of the Wadi Mugharid drama opened on a low key, with the elucidation of minor mysteries. The doctors at the Hadassah Hospital had firmly vetoed any attempt to question Toby until his condition was stabilized and he was out of danger. As Inspector Abrams chafed in increasing frustration at this further delay, various items of information came in to him which did little to improve his temper. For one thing the public prosecutor had ordained that unless Abrams brought some substantiated charge against Gregory Vadik, he would have to let him go. Abrams pleaded desperately for another forty-eight hours, and a further concession that Vashti Vadik should be kept from her husband during that period. After a great deal of argument he had grudgingly been given the stay. For another, Margaret Cochran, whom he was desperately anxious to question now that he had heard Penny's belated statement, had eluded him. Word had come from the Tel Aviv airport that she had flown out of there—destination London—the day of her flight from Jerusalem. Further, a member of the Israeli archaeological team, which had immediately descended in force on the Garden of Zadok, had stumbled upon the body of Valerie Pierson in her makeshift grave, and Abrams had had to endure much sarcastic comment from his superiors about archaeologists doing the job of the police.

Penny, now that Toby was safe if not exactly well, had regained much of her normal ebullience and deeply sympathized with the beleaguered inspector. To spare him further shocks she decided to tell him about the Jesus document. It did nothing to cheer him up.

"You mean there could be still *another* motive for the murders?" he grumbled.

"No, I'm almost sure not," Penny comforted, and explained that as well as she could.

As a matter of course, he checked her story with Maisler, who snorted at this further breach of secrecy but added a note which brought joy to Penny's heart. "The C-14 tests on the document confirm that it is in the right time range and undoubtedly came from the site at Wadi Mugharid, but, in view of the document's importance, police cooperation is requested in still keeping it under wraps until the government has officially taken over the site for further investigation," the little scientist informed him.

"What next?" Abrams sighed as he put down the phone. "Is there anything else you just happened not to have told me?"

"No, that's it," Penny said with relief. "Now you know everything that I know, and I'm thankful it's off my chest. So far as the murder goes, it was a red herring, just as the terrorist activity was. The motive first and last was Zadok's treasure."

"Well, I'm glad you are so certain," Abrams growled, "because I'm not."

The first gleam of light on his horizon dawned when a report came in from Sodom that two Arabs had been caught trying to slip across the border into Jordan; one of them was among the missing Arabs from the excavation site, the other a Jordanian Arab who decided he did not want to face an Israeli prison or perhaps worse, and volunteered to cooperate with the police for the price of his freedom. He claimed he had not been involved in the terrorist activities, but that he knew where the main party was hiding out in the wilderness. He also added another interesting item: several of the Arabs from the Wadi Mugharid dig had been forced to accompany the terrorists against their will and were, in effect, being held as hostages.

This complicated Abrams's plan of action, since he was desperately anxious for more than one reason to have all the Arabs from the dig alive and able to tell their tales. Unfortunately, the terrorists had chosen their hideout all too well. The series of caves were all but impossible to approach unseen, and when the surprise gas attack was mounted, Abrams's men did not have time to get into position after the tear gas was launched. The Arabs came out shooting, using their hostages as shields, and in the ensuing bloody gun battle, the carnage was heavy: one Israeli

soldier dead and three wounded, all the terrorists and all
the hostages dead, save one who had had the sense to fall
down as soon as the shooting started and play dead.

Abrams looked in grim despair at the bodies of the
three Arab youths that were found after the bloody
melee and wondered which one of them had been the
murderer's messenger; now he would never know. He
turned his attention to the sole survivor, who, when he
had recovered from his state of shock, gave the inspector
information which sent him posthaste back to the Wadi
Mugharid.

The collection of tents on their small plateau had taken
on the grim appearance of an internment camp, with police
Jeeps blocking the road and armed police patrolling the
muddy perimeter. Abrams broached the manmade barrier
and issued some quiet orders. He waited while these were
carried out. When his suspicions had been confirmed, he
turned to the sergeant in charge. "Where are they all?"

"In the mess tent, sir."

"Right. Four of you come with me and keep your guns
at the ready."

He marched into the tent and stood looking around the
long table. Goldsmith at the end of it was drunk, his eyes
unfocused and unseeing; Tahir was sitting in deep gloom
a little apart from the rest. The other three—Carter, Grayson and Ali—were all huddled at the bottom end of the
table, engaged in a dispirited card game. They glared at
him.

"About time you showed up," Carter snarled. "How long
is this nonsense going to continue? I demand that you
either charge us with something or let us go. We've stood
all we are going to—you're worse than bloody Nazis."

Abrams ignored him but with a slight nod sent his
policemen, two on either side of the card players. "Ali-
Muhammed," he said in a flat, even voice that showed
nothing of his inner anger, "I arrest you in the name of
the Republic of Israel on charges of organizing terrorist
activities against the republic and on the capital charge of
murder."

Ali started to rise from his chair, his face working.
"No," he muttered. "No, I did not kill anybody—you can't
prove it."

"Your men are all dead," Abrams went on inexorably, "but we have two witnesses who will testify to your activities. Take him away."

There was a slight scuffle as the policemen clapped the handcuffs on, and Ali started to writhe and scream. "You won't get away with it," he screamed as he was dragged out. "My country, all the Arab countries, will come and drive you Israeli pigs into the sea where you belong. We will bring freedom, freedom . . ."

Abrams kept a tight hold on himself as the shouting died away, then turned his attention back to the rest, who were sitting staring at him like so many stone carvings. "And I arrest you," he went on to Selwyn Grayson, "on charges of supplying arms and armaments to the terrorists and of complicity in their late activities."

The tall man surged to his feet. "This is a frame-up. Just because I work for a country that is hostile to Israel . . . I demand to see the American consul."

"I should tell you that the false compartments in your Land Rover have been discovered," Abrams said quietly. "And the arms taken from the dead terrorists, together with the testimony of my witnesses, will confirm their point of origin. After you are taken to Jerusalem, you will be allowed access to your consul, but I must warn you that since the charge will be a capital one, I doubt whether your government will wish extradition. Don't make it any worse for yourself than it already is by resisting arrest, either now or later. My men in their present jumpy state would have little compunction about shooting you." Still muttering, Grayson was handcuffed and led away.

Carter looked up, the beginnings of a smirk on his dazed face. "So it's all over! Good work, Inspector! I take it we are now all free to go."

"Not quite; not quite yet, Mr. Carter," Abrams returned. "There is still some unfinished business concerning the attack on Robert Dyke and the murder of Dr. Pierson."

The look of shock returned. "But you just arrested Ali for the murder!"

"I arrested Ali for the murder of Officer Baum and of the Arab hostages from the camp here who were killed by the terrorists. All except one, I should say. There may be further charges against him, of course."

"Which one escaped?" Carter said quickly.

"His name is Yusuf, I believe," Abrams said in a curious tone, and there was a deep-throated rumble from the corner in which Tahir was sitting. For the first time Abrams looked over at him. "In order to clear up matters, I must request you all to come with me to Jerusalem. This should not take long, and afterward you will be free to go. If you do not wish to return here, I suggest you take all your belongings with you now."

"Whassat?" It was Goldsmith's blurry voice from the end of the table. Abrams repeated what he had said. Goldsmith lurched to his feet. "Good, good! Gotta get out of here, gotta get away from here fast," he muttered thickly and stumbled out with an escorting policeman.

There was a short delay while the three remaining men got their gear together; a delay which Abrams put to good use. He radioed ahead to Jerusalem to have Gregory Vadik brought to the hospital and his wife from her hotel. Things were running smoothly at last, and he felt the time had come to play his final ace.

His plan was quite simple. With Ali and Grayson firmly tied in with the terrorists, he was virtually certain they were not involved in Pierson's murder—which left the remaining four men as suspects. He would first confront them with Robert Dyke, who he knew already could not identify his attacker. This should lull the murderer into a false sense of security. And at that juncture he would spring his big surprise.

The news of Tobias Glendower's rescue had been kept a complete secret from them; only Vashti Vadik knew, and she had been kept incommunicado from the rest. Their visit to young Dyke over, he would confront them with Glendower, either conscious or unconscious, and count on the shock to have its desired effect on the murderer. Even if Glendower were still in no shape to identify him, Abrams felt he could not lose out. There was no way any of them could escape from him now. So certain was he in his own mind that Gregory Vadik was the culprit that he felt almost sorry for the funereally silent trio of men as he rounded them up for the trip back. Goldsmith, who was still in sad shape, went with two policemen and Carter in Carter's car. Tahir went with the inspector and a constable; they were met at the hospital by another bevy of police escorting the still imperturbable Vadik. Abrams took the senior officer aside. "Where's Mrs. Vadik?"

"On her way from the hotel with Dr. Spring. They'll be here in a few minutes."

"Right, well, we won't want them in on this first part. When they get here, take them directly to the other room and wait for us there."

He led the quartet with an equal number of policemen to the room where Robert Dyke lay. The young man, his head still swathed in bandages, his face pinched and pale, looked startled as the group crowded into the tiny, cell-like room; the faithful Hedecai, ensconced in the room's only chair, looked equally so.

"Robert Dyke," Abrams said in a formal voice, "can you identify your attacker from this group of men?"

Robert, looking even more startled, shook his head and winced. "I'm afraid not," he said faintly. "As I already told another officer, I was bending down when it happened. I heard a movement behind me but before I could look up, the world caved in. I'm sorry."

Abrams contrived to look disappointed. "I see. I'm sorry too," he said stiffly and motioned the group out.

"Well, thank goodness it is all over," John Carter said with an explosive sigh of relief. "Can we go now?"

Gregory Vadik spoke for the first time. "I have been very patient. I have cooperated with the police in every way, but my patience is at an end," he rumbled. "I demand to be released and I demand to know what you have done with my wife and why I have not been allowed to see her."

Abrams held up a restraining hand. "In a moment, gentlemen, in a moment. Just one more stop and you will be free to go about your business."

Vadik drew himself up. "I demand to know where you are taking us now."

"To see your wife, for one thing," Abrams returned, leading them through the bustling corridors of the hospital.

"Something has happened to her!" The big man's voice was filled with sudden alarm.

"No, she is quite all right." Abrams stopped outside the guarded door and nodded to the policemen, who opened it.

The inspector motioned Goldsmith, Tahir, Carter and Vadik in that order to enter. He slid in quickly behind them and watched their faces as their eyes adjusted to the dim light of the shuttered room.

Sir Tobias Glendower, so festooned in bandages that he looked like a very clean mummy, lay on the bed, one leg hoisted high in the air in traction, his round face as serene as a baby's, his eyes shut tight. On one side of the bed stood Penny Spring, looking apprehensive; on the other Vashti Vadik, looking frightened, and as her husband entered the room, her eyes sent him a message of mute appeal.

As Tahir took in the figure on the bed, he let out a roar, "Glendower-*bey!*" and leaped toward it, only to be held back by two of the policemen.

Abrams was so concentrated on Vadik that he almost missed the definitive moment. John Carter took a step toward the bed, and before their eyes his polished veneer cracked and crumbled. His face an ashy white and working, he muttered, "It's a trick, a filthy trick. He's dead. I know he's dead. He must be dead." His voice rose hysterically.

Like a ventriloquist's dummy the round blue eyes under the heavy bandages popped open. "Afraid not, Carter," Toby said in a surprisingly strong voice. "You murdered both the Piersons, but you botched mine. There's your man, Abrams, and I can prove it."

Carter let out an inarticulate cry and made a dash for the door. His sudden rush took Abrams off balance and sent him reeling, but he was destined not to get far. Gregory Vadik stuck out a leg and Carter went tripping over it, sprawling across the threshold, where he was pounced on by two policemen. As they hauled him to his feet, he screamed into Vadik's face. "You won't get away with it. You're as guilty as hell. You're the man Pierson was waiting for. You're the buyer. You're to blame."

Abrams felt a surge of triumph. "Well, Sir Tobias?" he asked.

The round blue eyes looked hard at Gregory Vadik for a moment, then turned innocently onto Abrams. "Like you, Inspector, I like to deal in facts, and I do not know a single fact that links either Vadik or his wife with the murders of

William and Valerie Pierson or the attempt on myself. Carter is obviously hysterical. I haven't the faintest idea what he is talking about, and I am afraid that's all I have to say on the subject." And he closed his eyes firmly.

Abrams looked in exasperation from him to Vadik, in whose eyes a gleam of amusement appeared. "Am I free to go?" the bulky man inquired.

"For the moment, yes," Abrams snapped, and with a little cry of joy, Vashti ran into her husband's arms. "But you will have to remain in Israel until I have finished my inquiries." Vadik smiled grimly and went out, his arm around his wife's shoulders. "Get them all out of here," Abrams said in disgust. "The others are free to go, too. Take Carter away and charge him."

As they hustled Tahir out of the room, he called back over his shoulder, "*Getmis olsun,* Glendower-*bey!* I thought I had lost you, but all will be well with me now."

"Thanks, old friend," Toby rumbled. "Go to the hotel and wait for Dr. Spring. She has good news for you."

"I have?" Penny inquired when calm had returned to the dim room.

"You *will* have," Toby amended. "I'll fix it with Maisler to let Tahir continue on the site until he goes back to Turkey. They owe me that much."

"I suppose you know you've practically broken the poor Inspector's heart by letting Vadik off the hook," she reproved. "He *had* to be the buyer, you know; it's the only thing that makes sense."

Toby's eyes remained firmly shut. "I don't know that for a fact and I certainly can't prove it. Neither, I imagine, will Abrams."

"And, besides, Vashti Vadik is a nice little woman," Penny went on ironically. "And helped to save your life."

"That too," he agreed.

"Well, at least that makes some kind of sense, though I must confess the rest of it doesn't make much to me. I mean *why* in the name of heaven did Valerie ever call us in in the first place? That was sheer madness! Do you feel up to elucidating or shall we postpone it until vim and vigor return?"

"No, I feel fine," Toby said, but he kept his eyes shut. "I'd just as soon talk the whole truth over with you now, so that I can get it clear in my head how much of it I'll tell Abrams."

"You're getting as bad as I am," Penny observed, and got an outraged grunt in reply.

"The main threads, as I see it," he went on, "were overwhelming greed, stupidity and a pair of murderers at cross-purposes. Valerie *was* a stupid woman—she must have been not to realize Carter was a roaring homosexual! Anyway, I think it went like this. Bill needed her money for that dig, so he had to let her in on the treasure project. We know that he never intended to share it with her. But, with all his faults, Bill was not a bad man, so he made the mistake of insuring his life for a large sum in her favor, so that when he did take off and disappear with his girl friend, Valerie would not be left high and dry. His big mistake. He never realized that Valerie was as anxious to get rid of him as he of her and had what she thought was a willing replacement waiting in the wings. She was a greedy woman, Carter a desperate man. I think their original plan was to have Bill locate the treasure and then to do him in, and collect both the insurance *and* the money for the treasure information. I imagine Carter came out to keep a close eye on him, and they had worked out some sort of arrangement that when Bill 'disappeared,' she was to give the alarm, in order to put herself in the clear and above suspicion for the insurance.

"It was here that things started to go wrong because of the cross-purposes. Carter needed the money but did not want Valerie along with it. Unless he makes a full confession, which I doubt, we'll probably never know what triggered him to attack Bill too soon, but I would not be surprised if he had got wind of Bill's liaison with Margaret Cochran. Anyway, he attacked prematurely, before Bill had led him to the site, and then had to try to force the information out of him. Bill must have realized that Carter had no intention of letting him live once he had got that information, so he held out as long as he could, hoping vainly that someone, probably Vadik, would start looking for him. When he could not hold out any longer, he told Carter the location of the treasure scroll scrap, but evidently not the *translation* of it.

"In the meantime, as we know, Goldsmith had alerted Valerie to the fact that Bill had disappeared. She took that as the all-clear to go ahead with their plan and—well, you know the rest. I suppose she never thought for an instant that we would succeed in finding him. But this put the heat on Carter. He had to get rid of Bill before any of us, including Valerie, arrived. And here his luck ran out.

"Without the Bedouin who made their untimely entrance and immobilized the Jeep, and without Robert's sharp eyes, we might never have found the body, and Carter would have got away with it. He must have been living on the edge of an abyss from then on. One lucky break he had was that all of us were so damned anxious to spare Valerie's feelings that none of us told her of the torture—which would have aroused her suspicions, too, because this was not part of the original plan.

"Carter must have spun her some cock-and-bull story about the treasure, but when he failed to get the scrap translated (I imagine his boyfriend at the site was the errand boy for that), he put a new idea into her head: I was still sniffing around, even though the arrest of the Bedouin seemed to have put them in the clear on Bill's death, so why not use me to find the site and then get rid of me. And like a chump I fell for it." He let out a lugubrious sigh and fell silent.

"Well, you're not too good with the female of the species," Penny comforted. "I've always told you that chivalry of yours would be the end of you, one way or another, and it damn nearly was this time. But how about Vadik? Was he in on any of this?"

"I think, now that we know Grayson was involved in this other business, that Vadik *must* have been the buyer. How Bill contacted him or his employers, God knows, but they must have had a planned rendezvous of some kind. Vadik is a smooth operator, and he probably had a spy in the camp, so that when Bill went, he came along posthaste to find out what was up. But I doubt that he revealed himself. He was hanging back to see what developed and what I was up to."

"But what about all this business with him and the Arabs?"

"Vadik is a pretty notorious character in the Middle East. It must have been a terrible blow to the terrorists, who were using the camp as their base for this attack on the British delegation, when Bill's murder was discovered and it brought the police to the camp. When Vadik turned up as well, they must have thought he was behind it and were threatening him to clear out before their own plan went into action. Again, I have the feeling that Ali knew something of what Bill was up to and was doing some polite blackmail to cover his own activities."

"What an infernal mixup!" Penny sighed. "What do you think will happen now?"

"They'll probably hang Ali, and I doubt whether Grayson will get away with less than a long prison term. They may hang Carter, but again I doubt it. Imprisonment, I should think, and for a *very* long time, I hope."

"And Vadik, the most dangerous of the lot, will go scot-free," Penny murmured reproachfully. "Unless you change your mind and help our nice inspector."

Toby's jaw set in a stubborn line. "Without Vashti Vadik, my corpse would be rotting along with Valerie's in a dark cistern. Carter would have got clean away with the murders. All she had to do was sit tight and say nothing, and her husband could have collected his commission on the treasure book from his employers, whoever they are; her humanity overcame her devotion to her husband—which is very evident, as you must have seen."

Penny forbore to point out that Robert Dyke, the Israeli police and she had had some hand in his rescue too; there was no arguing with Toby in this mood. She changed the subject. "Oh, by the way, the mystery of Margaret Cochran is explained. I got a letter from her this morning. She said she could not face her drinking problem or her life here a moment longer. She flew back to her sister in England and is currently drying out in a clinic there. I think she'll be fine now." Toby grunted. "I suppose you'll be here quite a while," she went on, "what with the leg and presumably having to testify at Carter's trial. You do realize I am supposed to go to the States at the end of this week, as I arranged before we left England? I could cancel, if you like."

He waved a bandaged hand. "By no means. Go ahead! I'll be all right. They'll keep Vadik here for a while trying to pin something on him, so Vashti will be around to hold my hand and stroke my fevered brow."

"Well, really!" Penny snorted, and went out slamming the door, leaving her partner smiling faintly to himself.

EPILOGUE

Penny had enjoyed her visit to America tremendously. She had found her son in fine fettle, had relished the extravagant splendors of the Dimola wedding and was suitably braced to face both the coming Oxford term and the vagaries of the unpredictable Toby.

"How is he?" she asked their joint and long-suffering secretary and girl Friday, Miss Phipps.

Miss Phipps rolled her eyes to heaven. "Absolutely unbearable and impossible! I'm so glad you are back. He still has to use a cane, and what that has done to his temper!"

Duly warned, Penny went into Toby's office. He was sitting completely enveloped in a blue cloud of tobacco smoke, gazing blankly at his desk, which was swept, burnished and devoid of any traces of work in progress.

"I'm back and dying for news," she announced cheerfully, "but I've been keeping in touch through the papers, and congratulations on the way everything turned out!"

He snorted.

"They say that the Jesus document is starting a worldwide religious revival," she babbled on. "And Bill is getting all the credit. That *was* clever of you, Toby. I also saw that they are giving you the credit for finding Zadok's tomb."

"I tried to talk them out of it, but they wouldn't listen." He broke his gloomy silence.

"Well, you *did* find it, and it's another feather in your already befeathered cap. The government must be pleased, since this should help their detente with Israel. Are they giving you anything for it?"

"They would have given me a knighthood, but luckily I've already got one. The Royal Academy is giving me a gold medal, and I'm probably going to get an Order of Merit in the next Honors list." He made it sound like a cup of hemlock.

"Oh, that's nice." A small silence fell. "Have the Israelis found anything in the garden?"

He gave a mirthless laugh. "Yes, they found the silver bars in the cistern all right, but the garden kept its final secret. When they got to the book, they found that the blocked spring had backed up under the earth and water-logged everything; all that was left of it was a soggy mess of unreadable fragments. Wherever Vadik is, he must be laughing his head off."

"At least they know the Temple treasure is a reality now, so they can go on looking for the rest. Speaking of Vadik, how did the trials turn out? I could find nothing about them in the papers, and I'm sort of surprised to see you back so quickly."

Toby sighed heavily. "Ali was condemned to death. Grayson, after a lot of haggling, got off with fifteen years. Carter never came to trial. He was found in his cell with his wrists slashed by a razor blade two days before it started."

"A razor blade! How did he ever get it?" Penny said in a horrified tone, and stopped aghast as a sudden thought struck her. "Vadik wasn't around, was he?"

Toby nodded. "Yes. Abrams told me he'd had a final confrontation of the two, hoping that Carter's charges might break Vadik down. He swears he does not see how Vadik could have done it, but he is sure that he must have slipped Carter the blade. The man, apart from everything else, must be a super magician, but Abrams could not prove a thing."

"Well, perhaps it is for the best," Penny said awkwardly. She knew how Toby must be feeling. "Carter is dead, which he richly deserved to be, and it has saved the Israelis a lot of trouble and expense." He didn't answer. "You know, I've been thinking a lot about all this," she continued in desperation, "and I've come to the conclusion that you are absolutely right. We should stick to our own trade and not get involved in this investigating business anymore. I mean, it's just not for us."

"Wrong," he suddenly boomed out. "Quite wrong! I have had time to reflect on what happened to me in that cistern, and I am not the same man who went into it. Some of the things that occurred no one would believe; I'm not sure I believe them myself. But one thing I do know: I was spared, and spared for a purpose. And I do not think that purpose was solely to bring Carter to the judgment bar. If my services, imperfect as they are, are called upon again, I shall go on—and on and on, if need be. What you do is entirely up to you, but I am in this murder business to stay!"

Penny just gaped at him; for once in her life she could not think of a single word to say.